The window of the Gunsmith's room began to slide open . . .

His gun, which was hanging on the bedpost away from the window, quickly found its way into his hand. He turned quickly and, without hesitation, fired two shots at the window. A gun went off with a flash, the bullet imbedding itself in the floor as both of the Gunsmith's shots struck home. With a cry the gunman in the window dropped his gun and fell to the ground below . . .

Don't miss any of the lusty, hard-riding action in the Charter
Western series, THE GUNSMITH

And coming next month:
THE GUNSMITH #55: THE LEGEND MAKER

THE GUNSMITH

54

HELL ON WHEELS

J. R. ROBERTS

CHARTER BOOKS, NEW YORK

THE GUNSMITH #54: HELL ON WHEELS

A Charter Book / published by arrangement with
the author

PRINTING HISTORY
Charter edition / June 1986

ISBN: 0-441-30958-5

Charter Books are published by The Berkley Publishing Group,
200 Madison Avenue, New York, New York 10016.
PRINTED IN THE UNITED STATES OF AMERICA

To Henry Po, Miles Jacoby,
and Nick Delvecchio, my tickets out.

HELL ON WHEELS

ONE

Every time Clint Adams thought that his resting time in Labyrinth, Texas was becoming more and more pleasurable, and that maybe his wandering days were nearing an end, he would get the itch to travel again.

That was the case now.

He was seated in Rick Hartman's saloon, eyeing one of Hartman's new saloon girls with interest and sharing a drink with the proprietor, his good friend, at his private table.

"Are you getting an itch?" Hartman asked, following the Gunsmith's gaze.

The girl was a lovely redhead with short hair, a dusting of freckles across her nose, large pale breasts, and long legs. She was eyeing the Gunsmith back, obviously approving of what she saw.

"More than one kind," Clint replied.

"Ah, the itch to move has come upon you again," Hartman said, nodding. "I'll tell you a secret, Clint."

"What's that?"

"I envy you."

Clint tore his eyes from the young lady and looked at his friend.

1

"You envy me? Why?"

Studying the contents of his glass, Rick said, "You ride into town when you want, you leave when you want, you don't have anyone to account to but yourself—"

"And what about you?"

"Me?" Rick said, looking at Clint. "I'm stuck here. I've got people who work for me, who depend on me—"

"Bullshit."

"What?"

"You heard me. That's a bunch of crap and you know it. You've got no family here, and that's the only thing that could possibly tie a man down."

"I've got a business—"

"Which could run very well without you for a while. You've got a bartender who knows his business, girls who know what they're supposed to do, and a regular clientele who would behave whether you were here or not."

"What are you telling me? That I could get up and leave whenever I wanted without any consequences?"

"Oh, there would be consequences, all right."

"Like what?"

Clint started to get up from his chair to approach the young lady and said, "You might never want to come back."

Clint had been eyeing the redhead ever since he'd arrived back in Labyrinth three days earlier. Normally he wouldn't have waited so long to approach her, but the simple truth of the matter was that he had not been interested enough up until now.

He walked over to her and said, "Do you have a break coming?"

Her eyes widened slightly because she knew immediately what he was getting at and was somewhat taken aback by his directness.

"I could arrange it," she said, and then added, "if I had enough reason to."

"Maybe I can give you enough."

The redhead, upon hearing Clint's offer, decided that it was time for her to take a break, and the Gunsmith's hotel was as good a place as any to take it.

When they reached there, they wasted no time in undressing each other and getting acquainted.

Clint had been in bed with redheads before, but never with one with short hair. That was an odd thing to be thinking, he knew, when the hair he was presently involved with was not even on her head. Long red hair was something he liked very much. He decided that at a later date he would ask this girl why she wore hers as short as she did.

Just as soon as she quit screaming . . .

After Clint and the redhead—whose name was Sadie Collins—returned from his hotel, Clint saw Rick Hartman still sitting at his table, just as he had left him. Sadie went back to work and Clint walked over to his friend.

"Mind if I join you?"

"Be my guest."

"Thanks," Clint said, "I will." He signaled one of the other girls for a drink and mimed that it was on the house, taking Hartman's words literally.

"What's the matter with you?" he asked.

"I've been thinking about what you said."

"What did I say?"

Hartman looked at Clint and said, "That I should be able to leave any time I wanted to without my business going under."

"Well, you should."

"Ah, maybe . . ." Hartman said, draining his glass.

When the girl came over with Clint's beer, he said, "Bring me one too, will you, Alice?"

"Sure, boss."

Alice was a tall brunette, leggy and slim, just Hartman's type. In fact, she had been his regular girl for the past few weeks.

While they were waiting for Hartman's drink, a commotion started at the other end of the room where a poker game was going on.

"I say you're winning just too dang much for your own good," a man's voice complained.

"Can't win too much for my own good," another man replied.

"Well, I say you are."

"Ain't."

"Are."

"Ain't."

"You know," Hartman said, "if those two weren't brothers, I think they'd probably kill each other. One's always accusing the other of cheating."

"Who are they?" Clint asked as Hartman stood up. "Simmons' boys?"

"Burt and Blaine Simmons. Let me go and shut them up."

"Why not let them be?"

Hartman scowled and shook his head. "Bad for business having a couple of fellas arguing about cheating. I'll be right back."

Clint, seated with his back to the wall, watched Hartman start to cross the room, and then saw Blaine Simmons—the complainer, this time—rise from his chair, knocking it over, and reach for his gun.

Normally his first instinct would have been to draw his

own gun, but this time he sprang from his chair and charged across the room at Rick Hartman's back.

"Down!" Clint yelled, as much to everyone else in the place as to Hartman.

Blaine Simmons fired his gun once—ostensibly at his brother who was seated across from him. The bullet missed Burt by a foot and traveled across the room toward Rick Hartman. As Clint struck Hartman in the small of the back, the bullet went by, digging a furrow in Hartman's side. Had the Gunsmith not knocked him over, the bullet would have struck him dead center—with the operative word being *dead*.

"Damn it!" Hartman shouted as his side began to sting and bleed.

Clint rose, crossed the room, and, grabbing Blaine Simmons' gun hand with his left, hit the man in his stomach with his right. The man's hand opened, and as he slid to the floor, clutching his belly, Clint ended up with his gun.

He turned to face Burt Simmons, who was getting up, and said, "Don't, Burt."

"That's my brother."

"Then get him out of here before he shoots somebody else—like you."

Burt stared at Clint for a few moments and then eased his hand away from his gun and helped his brother to his feet. As they moved toward the doors, Clint returned to Rick Hartman's side, where Alice already was.

"How are you?"

"Ruined a good shirt," Hartman complained.

"He's fine," Alice said. "If you'll help me get him into his office, I can clean him up while somebody fetches the doctor."

''I do[...]d a sawbones!'' Hartman said.

''Shu[...] Clint said. He looked around, picked out a man, an[...]ucted him to get the doctor. After that, he and Ali[...]ed Hartman to his office, where Rick continued to [...] plain.

TWO

By the time Dr. Wells appeared, Alice had the wound pretty much cleaned up, and Wells simply examined the edges of it, spreading them with his fingers.

"Ow, damn it. Between you and this woman you're gonna kill me yet."

Wells ignored Hartman's complaints and said to Clint, "The wound is clean. He'll be fine." To Alice, he said, "Would you like a job as a nurse, young lady? I can use someone like you."

Alice looked interested and said, "I'll think about it."

"I'll just take a drink on the house as a fee, Rick."

"What else is new?"

"As long as you're in good humor, I know you'll be fine. Good evening."

After Wells left, Hartman put on his bloody shirt and said, "Alice, I think I'm ready to turn in. Would you like to meet me upstairs?"

Alice nodded enthusiastically.

Clint frowned at his friend. Hartman usually never turned in until the saloon was empty and he could close up personally.

"Be a good girl and go out and tell Silas that he'll be closing up tonight."

"Right, boss."

When she was gone, Clint said, "What's that all about?"

"I'll tell you in the morning. Join me for breakfast?"

"I was thinking of leaving—"

"Wait one more day and join me for breakfast. I think it will be worth your while."

Clint stared at his friend for a long moment, then nodded, and said, "All right. I'll join you for breakfast."

"Good. Right here at eight. Alice is a fine cook and I'll have her whip something up."

"Fine," Clint said, frowning at Hartman.

"What are you staring at?"

"Your head."

"Why?"

"You didn't hit it when I knocked you down, did you? Or catch a piece of lead?"

"My head is fine. Why?"

"Just asking," Clint said, moving toward the door and passing Alice on the way. "Just asking."

When Clint arrived at his room, he was not surprised to find his door ajar. No one who was waiting to kill him would have left the door open as a warning, so he assumed—and correctly so—that the person inside was not waiting to do him any harm.

As he walking in, he saw Sadie sitting up in his bed, naked and bathed in the soft light of the dim wall lamp. Her breasts were large enough to cast shadows on her own body, and the nipples were taut with anticipation.

"I hope you don't mind."

Clint closed the door gently, locked it, and, starting to undress, said, "I don't mind at all."

In his room above Rick's Place, Rick Hartman was being put to bed by Alice Chalmers.

"You need your rest," she said, pushing his hands away when he began to grope her.

"Hell," he said, reaching for her again. The move caused the tape over his wound to stretch his skin, and he sucked in a breath.

"See?" she said.

"Well, if you'd stop fighting me, it wouldn't happen. Besides, you've got to stay with me. We don't know what may happen during the night."

"Like what?" she asked skeptically.

"Who knows? But I might need you."

"Yes," she said after a moment, "you might."

She undressed, stretching her long, limber body for his benefit—before climbing into bed with him.

After they made love, she said, "I sense something . . . final in this."

Hartman raised his eyebrows. It had been his experience that when a woman thought she could read his mind it was time to go on to another woman. Maybe this was the final omen that the decision he had made was the right one.

"Not final," he said, holding her close. "I just—might be going away for a while."

"Why might?"

"It depends on what happens tomorrow at breakfast with Clint."

"I'll burn it."

"No, you won't. You're too good a cook to burn it even

on purpose. Besides, you want to impress Clint.''

"Do I?"

"Doesn't every woman?'' Hartman asked.

He knew how attractive Clint Adams was to women, whether because of his reputation or not. He did not hold that against Clint. They were friends and generally stayed away from situations where they might be sharing a woman. However, one of them taking up with a woman after the other was done was not against the rules.

"Not this woman,'' she said in a small voice, "but I won't burn the breakfast.''

Apparently Alice sensed that Hartman might be pushing her toward Clint Adams now. Maybe, he thought, she had detected something final, after all.

THREE

"Hell on what?" Clint asked around a mouthful of scrambled eggs.

"Let me explain this, all right?" Rick Hartman asked.

"Go ahead," Clint said, "I'm real interested."

"I thought you would be."

Clint had appeared at Rick's Place early that morning, and his knock had been answered by Alice herself, looking fresh and wide awake—and lovely, of course.

"Come on in, Clint," she said cheerfully. "I'm getting breakfast ready now. Sunny side up or scrambled?"

"Scrambled, Alice, thank you."

She let him in, locked the door behind him, and then went back to the kitchen. Rick Hartman was seated at his table with his back to the door. Two coffee cups and a pot of coffee were on the table. He had left the chair against the wall for Clint Adams. It was the one constant reminder between the two of what had happened after Wild Bill Hickok had been killed, and Clint Adams had crawled into a bottle because of it. It had been Rick Hartman who had shown the Gunsmith the way out of the bottle, and they had been friends ever since.

"Coffee strong?" Clint had asked.

"Take the skin off your palate," Hartman had replied.

After pouring a cup of coffee for Clint Adams, Hartman had asked his friend if he ever heard of a gambling train called Hell-on-Wheels. Now, he was going to tell him about it.

"It's up Omaha way. Ever since they started building the railroad west, towns have been set up at each railroad stop, and when work is completed on that section, the whole town picks up and moves on."

"What's that got to do with gambling?"

"I'm coming to that. The train that runs along that route is called Hell-on-Wheels because it offers every possible vice imaginable. Whores, gambling, con men—everything a man needs to make life interesting."

"How long has this been going on?"

"I heard about it a couple of months ago. I guess as long as there are people living along the route, until it's finished, the train will continue traveling back and forth, dropping off the suckers and picking up new blood.

Clint gave Hartman a frank look and said, "And which are we?"

Hartman smiled and said, "We're the new blood, my friend."

"Don't tell me you're thinking of leaving Labyrinth?" Clint asked, feigning disbelief.

"For a while."

"What brought this on?"

"Last night," Hartman said, frowning. "That idiot Blaine Simmons could have killed me right then and there. That's when I decided that at least once I'd get out of here and take a vacation."

Clint found that odd. He would have thought that the incident with the Simmons boys would have had the opposite effect on Rick Hartman, convincing him that he could *not* leave Labyrinth and his business.

"A vacation?" Clint said. "Checking out a gambling train? Sounds like a working vacation to me."

"We can have some fun, Clint," Hartman said. "Come with me. The action will be just the kind you're always looking for."

"What's that?"

"Cards instead of guns."

Alice came in with breakfast then, a spread that was large enough for four men. Clint and Hartman dug in, suspending conversation so they could concentrate on the steak and eggs and bacon, potatoes, biscuits, jam, and more coffee. When they were finished, Clint was the first to bring up the subject again.

"When do you want to leave?"

"Tomorrow morning. You can leave Duke and the rig behind, and we can catch a train at the railhead. A couple of changes along the way and we'll be in Omaha. All we have to do is follow the route until we find the train."

"How does the railroad feel about this?"

"From what I hear, they pretend to mind, but they don't. It keeps their men busy when they're not working, and it keeps them broke enough to keep going back to work. It works to everyone's advantage."

"And what's our advantage?"

"You and I know what we're doing around a deck of cards, Clint. There's got to be some high-stakes games on that train. What do you say?"

"I'm interested, but Duke's not going to like being left behind. Are you in some kind of hurry to get there?"

"Not in a hurry, I guess. Why?"

"I'd like to get you on a horse for a while. That'd really be a vacation."

"I'd rather take the train—"

"Then you explain it to Duke."

Hartman frowned. He did not get along with Clint's big black gelding and did not relish the idea of being alone in the livery stable with him. Clint insisted on talking about the damned animal as if he were as smart as a person—and sometimes Hartman thought Duke was.

"All right," Hartman said. "We'll go part of the way on horseback. How will Duke like traveling part of the way by rail?"

"He'll like it fine," Clint said, pouring more coffee. "After all, everybody needs a vacation once in a while. Right?"

FOUR

They met at the livery the next morning, and Clint picked out a handsome chestnut mare for Hartman, saying, "You have a way with women."

"Funny," Hartman said, "I was just thinking the same about you last night."

Omaha, Nebraska would have been a busy town even if the Union Pacific didn't start its trek from there to a point in Utah. The town was teeming with people from all walks of life—gamblers, whores, preachers, sinners, drummers, drifters, con men, and con women—half of whom seemed to be waiting for the now legendary Hell-on-Wheels.

Not all of them would get on, though.

As they rode through a light rain down a muddy main street into Omaha, Rick Hartman mentioned this fact to Clint Adams.

"What do you mean?"

"You have to qualify."

"Do we qualify?"

"We should."

"We should? You mean we came all this way and you're not sure?"

"Well, as long as I can find my friend—"

"What friend?"

"Pete Cross."

"Is he involved with his Hell-on-Wheels operation?"

"In a way."

"Are you being evasive with me, Hartman?"

"Not at all," Hartman said. "It's just that his role is very hard to define. Let's just say he's a ticket agent and leave it at that."

Neither of them had ever been to Omaha before, but Hartman said he thought they should stay at the hotel called Omaha House.

"Is that where we'll find your friend?"

"I doubt it, but it's a starting point. Let's put the horses up at the livery, first."

After doing that, they slogged through the muddy, busy streets of town to the Omaha House where they stamped as much mud off their feet as they could before entering.

"Is this the end of the rain?" Hartman asked the clerk hopefully.

"I'm afraid it's just the lull in the storm," the well-dressed, sweet-smelling clerk replied. "What can I do for you gents?"

"We'd like rooms," Clint said.

"Two?"

"Preferably," Hartman said. "My friend snores, and I've been known to invite a woman or two to my room for a late snack. The two don't go together."

"I would think not," the clerk said, straightfaced. He turned the ledger around so it faced them and said, "Please sign in."

"Of course."

Hartman's bantering did not surprise Clint. His friend had been in such a mood since leaving Labyrinth. It was as if being free of that town and the pressures of his business suddenly released a demon from inside him, a demon devoted to the enjoyment of travel and of life in general. The businessman was gone and the adventurous traveler had made his appearance.

It took some getting used to.

After they'd signed in and received their keys for rooms across from one another, they carried their own gear upstairs and agreed to meet in two hours, after some much needed cleaning up. They managed to miss each other in both the bathhouse and the barbershop, but they had obviously been to both those places, for when they met in the lobby, they were clean and clean-shaven. Neither, however, had opted for the proferred toilet water. The scent—or stench—of the one worn by the clerk was still fresh in their nostrils.

"This is your party," Clint said to Hartman. "What's next?"

"I don't know about you, but I'm hungry."

They both looked outside where the rain was coming down in solid sheets.

"Want to try in there?" Hartman asked, indicating the hotel's dining room.

Clint shrugged and said "As long as the waiters don't smell like the desk clerk."

During dinner they discussed their plans.

"Where does your friend live?"

"That's not generally known," Hartman replied, "but we should be able to get some information about him at a saloon called the Bull's End."

"Bull's End? Not Head?"

"No," Hartman said seriously, "the Bull's End."

Clint stared at his friend for a few moments and then shook his head. "Hell-on-Wheels and the Bull's End. I'm starting to think that maybe I made a mistake traveling with you. This new freedom of yours has made you dangerous."

"Don't worry," Hartman said with confidence, "you made the right choice. Just follow me."

"Many a massacre has been preceded by those words," Clint said ominously.

After dinner, Mother Nature seemed to have taken their side. The rain had let up just enough for them to make it to the Bull's End, at which time the sky opened up once again and began pouring rain down with a vengeance.

"What does that tell you?" Hartman asked.

"I don't know."

"That our hearts are pure and our mission is an honorable one."

Clint said, "I'm glad I don't read the same books you do."

"Let's get a drink."

The Bull's End was huge. In spite of its size, it was filled virtually from wall to wall. The only empty space in the place was a large stage where the entertainment obviously took place—when there was entertainment.

As they approached the bar, Clint saw—like a bad dream come true—the rear end of a bull suspended above it, hanging from the wall.

"See," Hartman said, "the Bull's End."

"I see it."

A couple of spaces opened at the bar, and they hurriedly filled them and ordered a beer each.

"Do you see your friend Cross?"

Hartman looked around for a moment, but gave it up as

futile. "There's just too many people in here," he said. "We'll have to ask."

Before Clint could stop him, Hartman had leaned over and asked, "Do you know if Pete Cross is in tonight?"

The bartender gave him a blank look. He said, "I serve drinks."

"Yeah, but I asked—"

"Forget it," Clint said, nudging him.

"But I only asked—"

"This is not Labyrinth, Rick, and we're not in your place where the bartender is friendly and helpful and courteous to all the customers. As a matter of fact, there aren't very many saloons like that."

"That says a lot for the kind of business I run, doesn't it?" Hartman said, half in jest and half with pride.

"Yes, it does, but if your friend Cross is not a pillar of the community, then asking for him in a saloon is asking for trouble."

"How do we find him then?"

"How close are the two of you?"

"Well, not real close. I know him. I've exchanged telegraph messages with him—"

"Wait."

Hartman had an extensive information system spread throughout the East and the West, one that he had put together largely over the wire. It had come in handy more than once for Clint, but now something occurred to him.

"You've never seen this man, have you?"

"Uh, well, no—"

"He's just one of your contacts, right?"

"Right."

"Great."

"How are we going to find him?"

"Well, you've already asked. If there's any problem

involved with that, we'll hear about it right here."

"So we stay here?"

"We stay here."

"I wonder when the entertainment starts."

Clint touched his friend's arm and said, "Do me a personal favor."

"What?"

"Don't ask more questions."

"Fine," Hartman said. "Hey, look."

Clint looked where his friend was pointing and saw a poker table with six chairs, one of which had just been vacated.

"Want to play?" Hartman asked.

Clint shook his head.

"It will be a change of pace," Hartman said.

"Be my guest."

Hartman picked up his beer and walked to the table. He said a few words, then nodded, sat down, and bought some chips. Clint was content to sip his beer and watch from the bar.

He was somewhat surprised by Hartman's apparent naiveté, but then the man had spent the last five or six years as a fixture in Labyrinth, Texas, never leaving, just building up his business and what was an informational empire. Why should he be acquainted with the etiquette of the trail?

Clint decided he was going to have to keep a very close eye on Rick Hartman and was actually starting to wish that the man had stayed in Texas.

FIVE

Clint knew they were in trouble when Rick Hartman started out by winning. It never looks good when a man walks in the door, sits down at a table, and immediately starts winning. What makes people even angrier is that he's a stranger, and the house is dealing, and they can't even accuse him of cheating because he never gets to deal.

So they sit and stew, and anger turns to frustration, which turns to an even deeper anger.

Clint picked the man out right away. He was seated directly across from Hartman—a large, beefy man with the red face and nose of a chronic drinker. Men like him wonder why they can't buy a card, never imagining that maybe by playing drunk they do buy the card, but never see it or never play the hand right.

The more he drank, the more he lost, and the more he lost to Hartman, the madder he got. By the time he was ready to do something about it, he was too drunk to be any real danger to Hartman, but he was drunk enough to be a danger to some innocent bystanders. If he started shooting, the place was crowded enough for it to turn into a disaster.

21

Clint, seeing all of this, began to circle to the other side of the table until he was standing directly behind the beefy, drunken, bad poker player. He suspected that the man was just as lousy a poker player sober as he was drunk.

The house dealer was doling out cards for a hand of stud, and Clint, watching Hartman, knew that his friend had a killer of a hand. He had an ace sitting on top, and Clint would have been willing to bet he had it wired to two more in the hole.

On the other hand, the drunk had a pair of kings in the hole and a queen on top, and he was feeling pretty good about it. The other three hands showed lower cards, and the dealer had a two of diamonds, the lowest card on the table.

"Ace bets," the dealer said.

"That's me," Hartman said unnecessarily. He took a blue chip from his pile and said, "Twenty."

The man to his right, sitting with a deuce, folded immediately. The next man called with his ten of spades, and that left it up to the drunk.

"Call and raise," the man said, tossing two blue chips into the pot.

The man on his left called with his jack of hearts. Clint figured the man for a pair, one up and one in the hole. The dealer called and looked at Hartman who simply called the raise. He was sucking the drunk in, making him feel that his hand was stronger than it was. The man with the ten called, and Clint figured that he was playing for a miracle.

"Coming out," the dealer said, dealing the second up card of the hand.

A queen fell on Hartman's ace, matching hearts. The beefy drunk made an annoyed sound from between his teeth. The miracle man bought another ten and apparently felt as if he'd bought his miracle. The drunk caught a jack and that seemed to mollify him a bit. His hand looked pretty, but it was still just a pair of kings. The last man watched a three fall on his jack and raised his eyes to the ceiling. The dealer paired up with deuces.

"Ace bets," the dealer said, and Hartman passed to the raiser. The pair of tens, however, had no such intention and tossed a blue and a white chip into the pot.

"Bet thirty."

"Raise," the drunk said immediately, matching the bet with a twenty-five-dollar raise and throwing chips worth fifty dollars into the pot. He was betting as if he had three kings already, which explained why he was losing.

The man with the jack and three folded, the dealer called, and that passed the play to Hartman.

"Call," he said, throwing in twenty-five dollars in chips.

The fourth player left in the game eyed the drunk speculatively and then raised ten dollars. It was a timid raise and the drunk recognized this.

"Your ten and twenty more."

Both the dealer and Hartman simply called as did the man with the pair of tens.

The next round of betting almost went by quietly. Hartman bought a low card and checked to the raisers; the tens were joined by a nine and checked; the drunk watched another king fall on top of his queen and jack and almost shit in his pants. The dealer gave himself a six of diamonds.

"Fifty," the drunk said, throwing a red chip into the pot. He was obviously miffed that no one had bet so he could raise.

"Call," said the dealer.

"Call," Hartman said, depositing his red chip in the center of the table.

"Call," the other man said in a strangled tone, still playing for a miracle.

The next round went the same way, with Hartman buying another low card and the ten catching no help. The drunk got a ten and now had an up and down straight on the table—ten, jack, queen, king—and two more kings in the hole. He was sitting pretty. He could pair up for a full house or catch the ace or nine for a straight. He could also catch a fourth king, which would have made him nearly unbeatable. The dealer bought a four of diamonds.

After two checks the drunk picked up two red chips and said, "A hundred."

The dealer cleared his throat and said, "There is a fifty dollar limit at this table, sir."

"Anybody object to raising the limit?" the drunk asked belligerently.

Hartman flexed his fingers and said calmly, "Fine with me."

The third player's eyes popped, but he said, "Whatever everybody else wants."

"I'll need my boss' okay, sir," the dealer said.

"Well, get it!"

The dealer motioned to an unseen person whose job it apparently was to go and fetch the boss whenever he was wanted.

Or she was wanted, as the case turned out.

A stunning, dark-haired woman who had apparently been poured into a blue-sequined, low-cut gown arrived at the table, gave Clint a casual look, and then said to her dealer, "What is it, Willie?"

"These gentlemen would like to raise the fifty-dollar limit to a hundred, Miss Delilah."

Miss Delilah looked over the hands on the table and said, "Looks like you got a corker going, Willie."

"Well, can we raise it or not?" the drunk said, still holding his two red chips.

The woman gave him a look of intense distaste and said, "Toss your money into the pot, friend."

"One hundred."

"Call," said the dealer. He had two deuces and the four and six of diamonds.

"Call," Hartman said, his face betraying none of the excitement Clint sensed was mounting inside of him.

The fourth player drummed his fingers on the table nervously until the drunk said, "Come on, come on!"

"Call," the man said, throwing chips into the pot in one convulsive movement. One blue chip stuck to his sweaty hand and he shook it free, watching it bounce and roll, making smaller and smaller circles on the table until it finally stopped and fell over.

"Last card," the dealer said and dealt. Clint and the woman exchanged a glance and then turned their attention back to the game.

"Ace bets," the dealer said.

Hartman hesitated a moment—a measured, deliberate hesitation—and then said, "I'll check."

"Check," the man with the tens said.

The drunk looked up at the woman who shrugged and said, "It's your money."

"Two hundred," the man said.

The dealer had his flush, Clint was sure, but was probably second best on the table because the drunk had bought another jack, filling him up. Hartman, Clint figured for aces full, the best hand on the table. The fourth player was way out of his league, probably milking three tens for all they were worth since the fourth one was on the table.

The dealer regarded his flush for a moment, looked at his boss, and then folded. Clint wondered how close he'd come to the straight flush.

The play went to Hartman now. Clint could see the tension in the drunk's shoulders as he waited for the man who'd been winning all night to make his play.

There was already a thousand dollars in the pot, and Hartman was ready to claim it and more.

"Your two hundred," Hartman said. With a look at the lady, he added, "And three hundred more."

The man with the tens stared in awe at the money in the center of the table. Realistically he must have known that he had no chance, but he had even less of a chance if he folded. He looked at the chips in front of him, spread them, and counted them. "C–call," he said, tossing in the chips and leaving himself with one lone, white chip.

The drunk stared across the table at Hartman and said, "Trying to steal the pot."

Hartman simply looked at the man and waited.

"All right," the drunk said, "your three hundred and"—he paused to count the remainder of the chips he had on the table and then threw them in—"a hundred and twenty more."

Hartman counted out his chips very carefully and said, "Call and raise—"

"I got no more chips!" the drunk exploded.

"I've g–got ten dollars left," the other man chimed in.

Hartman looked at both men and knew that if he bet fifteen dollars more they'd both be out of the game. Clint knew that if he did that the drunk would react very badly.

"In deference to the lady," he finally said, withdrawing his hand, "I'll just call. I don't want to be the cause of any trouble."

"Hell," the woman said, "if they can't pay the freight, they might as well go home."

Hartman exchanged a glance with her and then picked up one white chip and tossed it in.

"Raise ten dollars."

"C–call," the third player said, throwing in his last chip.

"I got no more chips," the drunk said again, very deliberately.

"Buy one," Hartman said.

"I got no more money."

"I'll take your chit."

"Damn right, you will," the drunk said. He groped through his pockets for a pencil and a piece of paper, found what appeared to be some sort of a receipt, and screwled his name and ten dollars on it. He threw it into the pot and turned his cards over without waiting for Hartman.

"Kings full!" he said triumphantly.

The third man simply turned his cards over, got up, and walked unsteadily to the bar.

"Ha!" the drunk said, reaching for the fat pot.

"Easy," Hartman said. He turned over his hole card to show three aces, which matched the fourth one on the table.

"Four bullets!"

"What?" the drunk said. "You had three of them all along and never raised?"

"No law against that," Hartman said, raking in his chips.

"Why you—"

When the man stood up and went for his gun, Clint was ready. He clamped his right hand down on the man's hand and said into his ear, "Don't be a sore loser."

The drunk was a beefy man going to fat, and although he was bigger than the Gunsmith, he couldn't move his hand.

"Leggo my hand!"

The woman moved her head and a couple of bouncers moved in behind Clint.

"I'm going to move my hand now," Clint told the man. "If you don't take your hand off your gun, these two bouncers are probably going to club you into the floor."

Hartman was not watching as he calmly stacked his chips carefully.

"He's got all my money," the man complained.

"If it wasn't him, it would be someone else," Clint said. "You're a lousy poker player, friend."

There was a tense moment. Then Clint felt the man's hand relax. He removed his own and the drunk's beefy hand dropped to his side.

"Escort this man to the street," the woman said to her bouncers.

Apparently, though, the man was too drunk to let it go. As he started to walk away, he suddenly whirled and drew his gun. Clint drew his and clubbed the man over the head with it. The two bouncers caught him very neatly as he fell and dragged him to the door as a path opened before them.

"Next deal?" Hartman asked, looking up.

"This table is closed, Willie," the woman told the dealer.

"Yes, ma'am."

"Can I buy you fellas a drink?" she asked Clint and Hartman.

"Both of us?" Hartman asked.

"You are together, aren't you?"

"Yes," Hartman admitted reluctantly, "we're together."

"Then both of you."

"We'd be delighted," Clint said.

SIX

"My name is Delilah Madison."

"Rick Hartman."

"Clint Adams."

They were standing at the bar, each holding a shot glass of whiskey that had been handed to them by the bartender.

"I suspect you saved me considerable trouble with your quick thinking," she said, "not to mention your quick move."

"I'm always ready to avoid trouble."

"Why didn't you kill him? You certainly could have. You're very fast."

"There was no reason to kill him. He was drunk and he'd lost all his money. Why ruin his day completely?"

She threw her head back and laughed, and both Clint and Hartman studied the smooth line of her neck. She was tall and buxom, and they felt that her body was just aching to burst from her dress, something they both would have liked to see.

"That's very good."

"He's a wit," Hartman said.

"What are you, then?"

"Me? I'm a gambler—"

"Sometimes," Clint added. "Rick owns a very fine saloon in Texas."

"Really?" she said, looking at Hartman.

"Nothing as elaborate as this, but I'm proud of it."

"I'm sure you should be." Looking at Clint, she asked, "And what do you do? Follow him around and keep him from getting shot by irate losers?"

"Not usually," Clint said, "but I do travel."

"A drifter?"

"I've done some drifting."

"And something else besides, I'd bet."

"This and that."

"You know how to avoid answering a question, too. That takes some practice."

"Some."

She gave up and asked a new question. "What brings you both to Omaha?"

"I'm looking for a friend of mine," Hartman said. "Maybe you know him, Pete Cross."

"Cross? He's a friend of yours?"

"You know him, then?"

"I know him, but I didn't think he had many friends." Her tone made clear how she felt about Cross.

"Actually, we're more acquaintances of Pete's than friends," Clint said. "Maybe you could put us in touch with him?"

"I doubt it," she said, putting down her drink untouched. She looked away for a moment, caught someone's eyes, and jerked her head.

"Why don't you gentlemen enjoy yourselves and have another drink on the house? I'm sure that Carla and Yvonne would like to help you."

Two women sidled up to them. A chunky blonde moved next to Hartman, while a tall, slender brown-haired girl bumped her hip against Clint's. Both were pretty enough, but couldn't compete with their boss.

"Keep them happy, girls."

"Uh, Miss Delilah," Hartman said as the woman started to move away.

"Yes?"

"Is that table opening again tonight?"

"That table? Not tonight, I'm afraid, but we have other games of chance you can try your luck at."

"I'm afraid I limit my gambling to poker."

"No other card games? Faro—" He stopped her before she could go on.

"Just poker."

"Well, there is another table in the back, but it's small stakes. I'm afraid that's all we have to offer right now."

"That's all right," he said. "Thank you for the drinks."

The woman moved away and the blonde bumped up against Hartman.

"I'm Yvonne."

"I guess that makes you Carla," Hartman said to the other girl.

"That's right," Carla said, "and we're a little thirsty."

"Now, why would you girls want to make us spend our money on watered down drinks?" Hartman asked, scolding them.

Yvonne shrugged smooth, pale shoulders and said, "That's our job."

"From what I just heard your job is to keep us happy."

"Well," Carla said, giggling, "we can't really do that down here."

"Well, this place looks like it has an upstairs."

"Oh, it does," Yvonne said. "Would you like to see it?"

"I'd be most anxious to."

"And you?" Carla asked, nudging Clint again.

Before Clint could answer, Hartman said, "My friend only goes sightseeing if it's for free."

"Oh, what a shame," Carla said, pressing small, firm breasts against Clint's arm.

"Yes, it is," Clint said, "but I'm real religious about my decision."

"I, on the other hand, am more than willing," Hartman said. "Ladies?"

"Both of us?" Carla asked.

"The more the merrier, I always say."

"Well," Carla said, moving away from Clint and taking Hartman's right arm while Yvonne linked her arm through his left, "let's go, then."

"Clint—"

"Go ahead, Rick," Clint said. "I might just check out that low-stakes game."

"Will you collect my money?"

"Sure."

"Well, then, there's nothing holding us here, ladies."

"Right this way," they said together, tugging him away from the bar.

Clint went to the dealer of the high-stakes game who was cleaning up the table and said, "My friend would like his money."

"Oh. You have to get that from Miss Delilah."

"And how do I do that?"

"Her office is that door in the back. See it?"

"I see it."

"Just knock and go in. She'll have the money."

"Just waiting for me, I suppose."

"Uh-huh."

Clint turned, walked to the door in question, knocked,

and entered in response to a called out invitation.

The room was expensively furnished, though small, and Delilah was waiting behind a desk that was almost as wide as it was long. Laid out on it were a couple stacks of money.

"All counted out?" he asked.

"To the penny."

Clint approached the desk and eyed the neatly stacked bills.

"Your friend did all right for himself."

"He had a hot hand," Clint said, picking up the money and tucking it away.

"You're not going to count it?"

"I trust you."

"That's very nice of you."

"Tell me, did you know it would be me coming to get it?"

"I didn't, but I hoped it would."

"That's why you didn't cash him in at the table."

"I wanted to talk to one of you back here—and I hoped it would be you. In fact, I figured it would be you."

"Well, that's very flattering. How did you figure I wouldn't go upstairs with one of your girls?"

"I can always tell a man who wants the best and doesn't want to pay for it."

"Meaning you?"

She stood up. Whereas another woman might have had to preen to impress him, she didn't have to.

"I have no false illusions about myself," she said. "I know what I'm good at and I know what my limitations are."

"What am I back here for, then?" he asked. "What you're good at or your limitations?"

"Does it have to be one?"

He stared at her and then said, "Do you have a bed here or do you want it on the desk?"

She looked a little startled and said, "There's no need to get crude."

"But there is a need to get truthful," he said. "How about telling me why you lured me back here?"

"All right," she said, "I'll tell the truth."

That remained to be seen, Clint thought, but he waited for her to continue.

"I was impressed with the way you handled yourself out there."

Clint did not reply.

"I need—I want to hire you."

"To do what?"

"I want you to find a man for me," she said. "And when you find him, I want you to kill him."

SEVEN

"Why?" Clint inquired.

"You don't have to know that," she said. "I'm hiring your gun, and a gun doesn't have a conscience, does it? It doesn't have to know why it kills somebody."

"You know a lot about it, huh?"

"Enough."

"What makes you think I'm a gun for hire?"

"Don't put me on, Clint," she said. "I saw you when you came in; I saw you work your way around behind that drunk. I can tell just by the way you walk."

Clint decided to let that go by.

"And then when I saw your move I knew."

"How are you going to pay for this?"

"I've already started," she said. When he frowned, she said, "The money in your pocket. You don't think that fourth ace was an accident, do you?"

"The game was rigged?"

"Only at the end."

"Your dealer's good," Clint said. "I didn't see where the ace came from."

"You weren't watching carefully. But, yes, he's good. You're good, too, aren't you?"

"Maybe."

"Maybe nothing. I only hire somebody who's good, the best if I can get him."

"Like me, right?" he asked, smiling.

"Yes, like you."

"So you think money is enough to make me kill somebody?"

"What else is there?"

"You tell me."

They stared at each other for a few moments, and then she got up and walked around the desk. "We can go upstairs," she said, taking his hand. "There's a back way."

"No."

"No," she repeated, frowning.

"Right here."

"Here?"

He nodded and said, "On the desk."

"On the—" she began, then stopped, and looked into his eyes. "You drive a hard bargain."

"On the desk."

"All right," she said with a resigned sigh, "Let me lock the door."

She went to the door, locked it, then turned, and leaned up against it. Her hands went to the bodice of her dress and undid a catch or a button. Her breasts bounced free, large and round, with big, distended nipples. Doing it on the desk excited her, he decided.

She worked the dress down over her broad hips and then kicked it away. She wore only a thin strand of silk then and dropped that to the floor. She was a big woman with wide hips, meaty, powerful thighs, and a belly just convex enough.

Naked, she walked across the room toward him, and he

felt the heat of her body before she reached him. She kissed him with her mouth open. She probed with her tongue and pressed her body against him. He could feel her nipples right through his shirt. Her hand snaked down between them and found the bulge in his pants, kneading it.

"Can we take this off?" she asked, indicating the gunbelt.

"As long as we keep it within reach."

"Of course."

He undid the gunbelt and put it on the far end of the desk, where he could reach it but where it wouldn't be in the way.

She opened his pants and pulled them down around his ankles. His erection sprang up and she captured it in both hands. She got down on her knees and began to lick it up and down lovingly, cradling his balls, sucking the head, and then drawing as much of him as she could inside her silky mouth.

She began to suck him then and he stood on his toes and cradled her head in his hands. Her head bobbed back and forth, and she reached behind him to cup his ass and draw him closer.

"Jesus," he said. Then when he could stand no more, he added, "Wait . . ."

He grabbed her and pulled her to her feet. Then he reached behind her to cup her cheeks. She was a big woman, but he lifted her and placed her on the desk top.

"It's cold," she whispered, but he silenced her with a kiss.

Her breasts were against his chest. He slid his mouth down over her chin, along the line of her neck, and into the valley between them. One at a time he found them with his tongue, circling her nipples and then drawing them into his mouth and suckling them until they were huge. She moaned and pulled his head close to her. She wrapped her legs around his hips. He stood up straight so that he could probe her with his cock, pushing and entering her easily.

Her breath caught in her throat and her nails raked at her back. He reached past her with his hands and cleared the desk, pushing everything to the floor. Then he pushed her down on it with such force that her hair, pinned up until that point, suddenly came loose. He began to plow into her, pushing her to the edge of the desk so that her long hair hung down on the other side of it. The desk was unyielding and allowed for maximum penetration every time he drove into her, bringing a gasp or a moan of pleasure from her each time. Her thighs were strong and squeezed his waist. Her heels were hard as they dug into his buttocks.

He pounded away at her with no thought whatsoever of her pleasure, and ludicrously, as he came, he wondered how Rick Hartman was doing.

Hartman was on his back, almost completely covered by flesh.

The blonde, Yvonne, the chunky one of the two, was seated astride his face, crushing herself against his mouth. His tongue was as deeply inside of her as he could get it, and her muscle control was such that at times he thought she was going to tear it out.

The other girl, Carla, taller and slimmer, was sitting across his hips with his cock buried inside her. She was riding him up and down.

It had become clear to Hartman early on that the two women worked together before and thoroughly enjoyed it. In fact, they had put on quite a show for him, hugging, kissing, feeling, licking him until both of them experienced huge orgasms, his erection becoming huge and pulsing, like something alive.

Then, on the bed, they had attacked him with their hands and mouths even more eagerly than they'd done before. They teased and tortured him, stopping him just short of coming everytime he was near the brink, and then finally they mounted him in the present fashion.

Carla was riding him up and down, doing all the work. Yvonne, a knee on each side of his head, was apparently trying to suffocate him. Both women had their eyes closed and their heads thrown back and achieved their orgasms at the same time.

Hartman came and had no idea that he was doing so almost in unison with the Gunsmith. Unlike his friend, though, he had no thought whatsoever about Clint Adams. In fact, his own climax was so intense that he had no conscious thoughts at all.

"Jesus, my ass is sore," Delilah said, sitting up on the desk.

"Don't be crude," Clint said, pulling his pants up and reaching for his gunbelt.

"You'd be something in a bed, you know?" she said, sliding off the desk. They had left it sticky and wet, and she was going to have to clean it before she did regular business on it again.

"Not me," he said. "I'm a desk man all the way."

"God," she said, walking across the room to pick up her dress.

He watched her smooth, well-muscled ass as she walked across the room, bent over, picked up the dress, and slipped into her dress with her back to him. When she turned, she was all buttoned up, and the only inkling anyone might have had that she had been undressed at all was that her hair was loose.

"You've got a good, strong desk," he said. "Maybe you should use it like that more often."

"I don't think so," she said, walking past him to get behind it again. She regarded the sticky mess on it for a moment and then looked at him. "I suppose you want to know who I want killed."

"Not really."

"His name's John Rogers."

"I'm not interested, Delilah."

"Why not?" she asked, frowning.

"Because my gun isn't for hire."

"But we just—"

"Yes, we did, but I never said I'd hire my gun out to you," he said, moving toward the door. "I'm not a killer for hire, lady, despite the way I walk."

He went through the door, shut it behind him, and then heard something shatter as it struck the other side.

Clint was standing at the bar fifteen minutes later when Rick Hartman came downstairs. He was somewhat surprised that Delilah had not had him thrown out of her place, but maybe she simply recognized a good con when she saw one and decided to accept it.

And maybe a cow's end could fly. Delilah Madison did not strike him as the kind of woman who would forgive being taken.

"Still holding up the bar, I see," Hartman said.

"Yep, still here."

"Find any action in the low-stakes game?"

"Nope."

"Find any unencumbered ladies floating around?"

"Nope."

"Find anything at all to do while I was gone?"

"Nope."

"I don't suppose you found Pete Cross while I was gone."

"Nope."

"You're damned talkative tonight, aren't you?" Hartman then hurriedly added, "No, don't answer that. I think I can figure that one out for myself."

"I think it's time to turn in and try again tomorrow, Rick."

"I think you're right. For some reason I find myself somewhat fatigued."

"Yeah."

They had one more drink and then started for the door, Clint still waiting for Delilah Madison to come out of her office with a shotgun.

"You know," Hartman said outside, "I think I'd better go and see the sheriff in the morning."

"What about?"

"Those two young ladies who took me upstairs."

"What happen? They take your wallet?"

"No," Hartman said, grinning, "but I think they just tried their damndest to kill me!"

EIGHT

During the night two men escaped death—one by skill and instinct; the other by pure, dumb luck.

Clint Adams could count on the fingers of one hand the times in his life he had truly been fast asleep.

Luckily, this night had not been one of them.

When the window of his room began to slide open—most assuredly not of its own accord—he came instantly awake. His gun, which was hanging on the bedpost away from the window, quickly found its way into his hand. Now, Clint felt that he was perfectly within his rights to assume that anyone coming through his window in a strange town was not a friend, and he was perfectly within his rights to assume that this person meant him harm. Now, these assumptions gave him every right in the world to shoot that person dead.

Which is exactly what he did.

He turned quickly and, without hesitation, fired two shots at the window. A gun went off with a flash, the bullet embedding itself in the floor as both of the

Gunsmith's shots struck home. With a cry the gunman in the window dropped his gun and fell to the ground below.

Rick Hartman, in his room across the hall, heard the shots and jumped up. By doing so, he banged into the man who had already entered his room and had been creeping closer to the bed to be sure he'd get a killing shot. The man, totally unprepared, staggered back toward the window, struck the sill with the back of his knees, and fell through the open window—which was only open because he had left it so.

One by skill and instinct . . .

One by blind luck . . .

The sheriff questioned both of them in Clint's room because that was where the shots had come from.

"And you don't have any idea why someone would be sneaking into your rooms?" Sheriff Casey McDade asked. McDade was a man in his early fifties and had shown up at the hotel with three deputies in tow. Of the three, one was now in the room with him, while the other two were seeing about cleaning up the mess on the street.

"Robbery's the only thing I can think of," Clint said.

The lawman looked at Hartman who said, "That's all I can come up with."

"Anybody have any reason to know that you fellas had money?" the sheriff inquired.

"My friend here had a hot night at the poker table in the saloon," Clint said.

"Which saloon?"

"The Bull's End."

"High-stakes game?"

"Fairly high," Hartman said.

"That probably explains it, then. Can't hold a man for defending himself, can I?"

"Guess not," Clint said, and Hartman nodded his agreement.

"I can leave a deputy on duty outside the hotel, if you like."

"That won't be necessary. We can take care of ourselves."

"Yep, I guess you can," the lawman said. Then he looked at Clint and said, "You should take a lesson from your friend here, though."

"How's that?"

"He took care of his man without firing a shot." The sheriff looked at Hartman and said, "That's admirable, son, real admirable."

"I appreciate that."

"Well, I'll let you fellas get to sleep, then. Before you leave town, you might want to stop by my office and sign a statement, so I can show it to the judge."

"We're not leav—" Hartman started to say, but Clint cut him off before he could go any further.

"We'll do that. We'll sure do that, right after breakfast."

"That'll be fine. Sorry you fellas had such a rude welcome in Omaha."

"Can't blame all of Omaha for the actions of two thieves," Clint said.

"Well, that's right nice of you to say."

After the sheriff and his deputy had left, Clint and Hartman watched from the window while the two men were carried away, both dead, one from two bullets and the other from the fall.

Clint shut the window and turned to Hartman who had

seated himself on the bed.

"What do you think?" he asked.

Hartman shrugged. "You're more experienced at getting shot at than I am. Think they were after the money?"

"If they were, why didn't they just break into your room? Why mine, too?"

"I don't know. Maybe they figured we'd split it."

"Will we?"

"Hell, no."

"Well," Clint said, "if they weren't after the money, what were they after?"

"Anything else happen tonight?"

"Well," Clint admitted, "something . . ."

He told Hartman what had happened between him and Delilah Madison.

"You dog. You were going to keep that from me, huh?"

"I don't kiss and tell."

"Well, I guess it's fair to think that she might have sent them after you for revenge, but why me?"

"Because we're together," Clint mildly suggested.

"We're not that close. Why'd she want you to kill?"

"I don't know."

"Weren't you curious?"

"Not really. I was too busy being insulted."

"Insulted. About what?"

"She said I walked like a killer. I don't walk like a killer, do I?"

"I don't know. I never watched you that close. Walk for me."

"Never mind. Why don't you go back to your room and get some sleep?"

"Good idea." Hartman got up, walked to the door,

then turned, and asked, "You don't think anyone else will try to kill us tonight, do you?"

"I doubt it, but if someone does, just take care of him without firing a shot. That was admirable, real admirable."

"Oh, shut up."

NINE

During breakfast the next morning in the hotel's dining room, they went over the possibilities again and then added a few more.

"What about the sore loser?" Hartman asked. "He might have been mad enough to try it."

"I don't think so. On top of having been clubbed over the head, he was drunk. I don't think he could have—well, wait, he didn't have to climb up to the window, he just had to have two persons do it for him."

"Right."

"But would they do it for free?" Clint asked, taking it one step further. "I don't think he has those kind of friends, Rick. And he didn't have any money left to hire them."

"Here's another possibility for you."

"Go ahead."

"Pete Cross."

"He'd try to have you killed?"

"He doesn't know it's me," Hartman explained. "All he might know is that a couple of men were asking for him in the saloon."

51

"And he'd send two men to kill them? What kind of friend do you have?"

"Acquaintance, remember? And I don't know—maybe he would."

"Look," Clint said, trying a new tack, "we don't seem to be very popular in this town. Why don't we just see if we can find your good friend Pete Cross today and then get on that Hell-on-Wheels train and get out of here."

"All right, I'm for that, but where do you suggest we start looking?"

"Where's the first place we're going this morning?"

Hartman thought a moment and then said, "The sheriff's office to make out statements."

"Then that's where we'll start."

"Pete Cross?" the sheriff asked. "You're looking for Pete Cross?" His tone made it plain what he thought of anyone who might be looking for Pete Cross.

"You know him?" Hartman asked unnecessarily.

"Oh, I know him," the sheriff said, and he didn't look particularly happy about it. "I know Pete Cross much better than I'd like to.

They had finished filling out and signing their statements and had asked the sheriff about Pete Cross just before leaving, making it seem as if it were just an afterthought.

"Is he a friend of yours?" the sheriff asked, obviously trying to classify them.

"A friend of a friend asked us to look him up while we were here," Clint said.

"Well, take my advice and stay away from him. He's bad news."

"Well, our friend was really pretty insistent," Hartman said.

"I thought you said it was a friend of a friend?"

"He was insistent, too," Clint said.

The sheriff gave them each a look that said they had both been classified in his eyes and that the classification wasn't good.

"Well, you can ask for him at the Bull's End or at a saloon at the other end of town. Just don't think he's gonna come looking for you with open arms. If you asked for him last night, I wouldn't be surprised to find out that he sent those two jaspers after you."

The other end of town was parlance for the other side of town, the seamier side.

"What's the name of that one?" Clint asked. "The other saloon?"

"The Bucket of Blood."

"Oh, fine," he said under his breath. "Thanks a lot, sheriff."

"When are you two gentlemen planning on leaving town?"

"The sooner the better," Clint said.

"Sooner suits me."

"We hear you."

As they left the sheriff's office, Clint said, "I don't suppose the saloon would be open this early."

"We're talking seamy, my friend," Hartman reminded him. "It'll be open."

"Well, I'm telling you one thing right now," Clint added, "if they have a bucket of blood hanging over the bar, I'm leaving!"

TEN

The seamier section of town existed on a different plane from the rest of the town. For one thing, their routine was not dictated by the clock. That is, the saloon stayed open all day and all night, serving drinks no matter what time it was. Had the sun not been shining so brightly, the activity in that section would have made you think it was after dark.

"Time stands still," Clint said as they walked down the street toward the Bucket of Blood. "It's always midnight over here."

"Yeah. We're more likely to find Cross in this area than anywhere else."

"I'm starting to think this Hell-on-Wheels is not such a good idea."

"It'll get better."

"Why don't we just go to the railroad clerk and ask him about it?"

"He'd probably lie."

As they approached the Bucket of Blood, they could hear piano music from inside. Entering, they found just a few people present, including the bartender and a little man playing the piano.

As they entered, the piano player stopped, turned, and faced them.

"You fellas looking for a game?"

"Not right now," Clint said.

The man, obviously doubling as piano player and dealer, shrugged, turned, and resumed playing his tune right from the point he'd left off.

The Bucket of Blood was ten steps down from the Bull's End. It was not as big and had no gaming tables and no stage for entertainment. The floors were dirty, the walls were dirty, and the tables and chairs were suspect, requiring a testing of their strength before anyone sat in them.

As they approached the bar, Clint looked above it, and sure enough, there was a bucket hanging from a nail on the wall.

"Want to bet?" he asked Hartman.

"Not a chance."

They ordered a beer each from the bartender, a very tall man in his forties with sallow skin and dark circles under his eyes.

"Cold or warm?"

Clint frowned and asked, "Who'd want warm beer, especially in the morning?"

With a bored look, the bartender said, "In this part of town you learn to ask. People have funny tastes."

"Cold," Hartman said.

"Comin' up."

The bartender drew two cold beers and set them down in front of them.

"Four bits."

"A little steep, isn't it?" Clint asked.

"That's the going price here. Want it cheaper, go

across town, but you'll have to wait a few hours for them to open to get it.''

"I see," Clint said, paying the man.

"We're looking for a friend of ours."

"Don't know him."

"We haven't told you his name," Clint said.

"Don't matter. I still don't know him."

Clint looked at Hartman and said, "He's got a very antisocial attitude."

"Maybe we can change it."

Clint looked at the man and said, "Look, friend, somebody tried to kill us last night, and it's put us in a very bad frame of mind. Now, I don't mind being overcharged for beer, but I would like to go ahead and ask my question before I'm told no. Understand?''

Unimpressed, the bartender said, "So ask."

"We're looking for Pete Cross."

"Don't know him."

What Clint did next surprised Hartman, but he recovered quickly enough to go along with it.

Clint threw his beer in the man's face and then grabbed him by the collar and pulled him halfway over the bar. Hartman took out his gun and inserted the barrel in the man's right ear.

"Now, I'm going to ask you again, real slow, and I want a better answer," Clint said in the man's left ear. "Do you know Pete Cross?''

"You guys are crazy—"

"Comes with the territory, friend."

Hartman said, "Answer the question," and screwed the barrel of his gun deeper into the man's ear.

"All right, all right," the man stammered, "I heard of him."

"He comes in here, doesn't he?"

"Once in a while."

"Well, I'll tell you what we want," Clint said, twisting the man's collar so that he was cutting off some of his air. "We're going to take our beers and sit at a corner table. If Pete Cross isn't here within the hour, we're going to take this place apart and you with it. You got it?"

The man nodded convulsively, and Clint released his hold so he could breathe.

"Now, I'm going to need another beer because I seem to have spilled mine."

"Cold or—" the man started to ask automatically, but then he hurried to the other end of the bar, drew a cold one, and returned with it as quickly as he could.

"We're going to sit over there," Clint said. "If I see an unfriendly face walk through those doors, I'm going to put a bullet right between your eyes."

"I got to leave to go get—"

"Send somebody," Clint said. "You're staying behind the bar until we see Cross."

"I don't have anybody—"

"Send the piano player. I don't like his music, anyway."

The man hesitated and then nodded.

Clint and Hartman walked to a corner table from where they could see the whole room. They each tested their chairs before sitting in them. They found that the table wobbled due to one shorter leg.

"You're mean, aren't you?"

"I'm not enjoying my stay in this town," Clint said. "Besides, it was you who took out your gun and stuck it in the man's ear, not me."

"Well, I knew you wouldn't, and I wanted to make sure that our friend didn't take you apart."

"I appreciate your confidence."

"Anytime."

"By the way, you'd better clean your gun. I'm sure the barrel's so stuffed with shit that it'll explode the first time you try to fire it."

Hartman actually started to reach for the weapon before he realized that Clint was kidding.

They both watched as the bartender called the piano player over and spoke very quickly to him, waving his arms in the air as he did. The little man looked over at them, nodded, and then left.

"Now he's going for an army of cutthroats that will either shoot us full of holes or pound us into the floor," Hartman said.

"Hold that thought."

"Ah!" Cross said. Apparently they had chosen a subject he was fond of.

"You looking to take a ride?"

"That's right, but I hear we've got to qualify."

"Well, you qualify," Cross said, spreading his hands and smiling. Clint noticed that the smile did not extend itself to the man's eyes.

"How do we get on?"

"I'll arrange it."

"For how much?" Clint asked.

"For you fellas, nothing."

"For us?" Hartman asked.

"Well, actually, that's the going rate," Cross said. "You see, the marks—excuse the expression—usually lose enough on board for us—ah, them—to be able to do away with the ticket price."

"I see."

"And what's your connection with the train?" Clint asked.

"Me? I'm just a sort of ticket agent. Yeah, see, I make sure they have your names, and you're in—or on, right?"

"Right," Hartman said.

"When?" Clint asked.

"You're in luck. The train is due to stop in here tonight."

"Tonight?"

"Midnight."

"A midnight stop?" Hartman asked.

Cross nodded. "The clerk goes off duty at eleven thirty, and the train rolls in at midnight."

"How many passengers will it be taking on?" Hartman asked.

"Enough to make stopping worthwhile. Besides, it will

have to let the other marks—excuse me—off. Will you fellas be ready?''

"We'll be ready," Clint said. "We'll also have a couple of horses with us."

"Can't do that," Cross said, shaking his head. "Sell your horses and leave them behind. It'll give you more money to play with."

Clint leaned forward and said, "I've got enough money to play with and I don't sell my horse."

Pete Cross stared at Clint Adams for a few seconds and then averted his eyes.

"No, I guess you don't," he said, which just confirmed for Clint that the man knew who he was. "I guess I can work it out for one horse."

"One's enough," Hartman said. "I can sell mine and pick up another when we get off."

Cross tried a smile and said, "If you can afford to after you get off."

"Oh, I'll be able to afford it, Pete," Hartman said. "You just get us on."

"You got it," Cross said, standing up. As he was about to leave, he turned and asked, "How'd you happen to know about the Hell-on-Wheels?"

"I've got more sources of information than just you, Pete."

"Yeah, I guess you do."

"How will we know that you've made the arrangements?" Clint asked.

"Just be at the train station at midnight," Cross said. "I'll make the arrangements."

He started for the door, then stopped again, and turned to them again. "About those two fellas you talked about, the ones who tried to shoot you in your sleep?"

"What about them?" Clint asked.

"They weren't from me. I didn't even hear that you were looking for me. I don't, uh, go to the Bull's End much anymore."

"All right," Clint said, which may or may not have meant that he believed him.

"No, I mean it. Look, where are they now?"

"The undertaker's, I'd say."

"I'll go and take a look at them. I may be able to tell you who they work for before you leave."

"Well," Clint said, "we'd appreciate that information, Pete."

"No trouble," Cross said. Then he looked at Hartman and said, "That money you send comes in real handy sometimes. I wouldn't want you to lose faith in me."

"I hear you."

Cross reached the door this time before he turned again to speak directly to Clint. "Uh, *you* may have one problem that you didn't anticipate."

"What's that?" Clint asked.

"They collect all guns from anyone who gets on."

Clint stared at the man until Cross got nervous, turned, and left. After that, Clint turned his eyes to Hartman, who also got a little nervous.

"He knows who I am, which means that the people who run this Hell-on-Wheels will know who I am," Clint said slowly. "I'm supposed to get on a train with gamblers, con men, and cutthroats, *and give up my gun*?"

"That wasn't in my information."

"Well, thank you very much," Clint said. "I guess you should have gotten your information right from Cross."

"Don't worry about it," Hartman said. "We'll figure something out."

"*You'd* better."

Something dawned on Hartman right then and there, though, and he said, "I may already have."

TWELVE

At precisely midnight Clint and Hartman—and about twenty others—were standing on the platform at the train station with their saddlebags over their shoulders. From what Clint could see there were about six or seven women among the waiting people, but one in particular caught his eye—not because she was the most beautiful or the sexiest, but because she was the youngest, barely eighteen if he was any judge. She was blond, about five feet seven. She had soft, gentle curves and was carrying a single piece of luggage—a floral-patterned carpet bag. He wondered what such a lovely young woman was doing getting on a train like Hell-on-Wheels.

"I see her, too," Hartman said, following his friend's gaze. "She'll probably be the highest priced whore on the whole train."

"Cynical bastard that you are, you're probably right."

"You know, given the crowd that's here it's a wonder the railroad denies the existence of this train. They could make a fortune selling tickets."

"It wouldn't be as exciting," Clint said, "and they wouldn't get the same number of people. These people would find somewhere else to go for their excitement.''

"I guess you're right. Come on, we'd better get down to the other end where the livestock car is.''

"Right," Clint said, picking up Duke's reins.

"You know," Hartman said as they walked, "it's probably just as well that they know who you are.''

"Why?"

"Well, they don't know you as the gentle, loving man I do," Hartman said. "They know you as the cold-hearted legend, the Gunsmith.''

"Which means?"

"Which means that Duke will probably get better treatment on the train than any of the people on it.''

Clint thought a moment and then said, "Well, all right, you may have a point there, but I'm still not getting on without a gun.''

"Did you do what I told you?''

"I did.''

"Then don't worry.''

Out of the darkness there was suddenly a bright light, and Clint realized that the train had approached at low speed with no whistle or light and now had suddenly turned its front light on.

"There it is.''

"There's an eerie feeling about this," Clint said.

"Like I said, it just adds to the excitement.''

The train pulled into the station very slowly, and when it finally stopped, several of its doors opened. It started belching forth people. Most of them were mumbling to themselves, while one or two at the most seemed to be fairly satisfied.

"Got to let one or two win to suck the others in," Hartman said.

"Spoken like a true saloon owner.''

The door of the livestock car opened and a ramp came down.

"You the fella with the horse?" a voice called.

Clint bit back a sarcastic reply and said, "Yeah, that's me."

"Well, bring him on up. We ain't got all night."

Clint walked Duke up the ramp. Hartman brought up the rear. A well-dressed man appeared from the darkness of the car and spoke to the man who had called out to Clint.

"A little more courtesy, Jack, we've got a celebrity in our midst. That's quite an animal you're got there, Mr. Adams. I don't blame you for insisting you be allowed to bring him along."

"The decision to allow it was yours, I assume?"

The man executed a slight bow and said, "My name is Hargrove, Emerson G. Hargrove. I have the honor of making some of the decisions aboard this train."

The man called Jack accepted the reins from Clint and looked Duke up, down, and sideways.

"Damn fine animal."

"Treat him like one," Clint said.

"Don't worry," the man said, "I ain't never mistreated a horse and I ain't about to start with this one."

"Make sure this animal receives very special care, Jack," Hargrove said.

"Don't have to be told that," Jack muttered.

"We can connect with the other cars through here, gentlemen," Hargrove said. "Please follow me."

As Hartman came abreast, Clint said, "I guess your friend Cross pulled a few strings."

"Of course," Hartman said. "We're friends, aren't we?"

At the end of the livestock car, Hargrove opened a door.

They stepped out and into the next car where he opened another door, admitting them to a small alcove. Inside, he turned to face them.

"I'm afraid I have another decision to make here, gentlemen."

"And that is?" Clint asked.

"It's the policy of Hell-on-Wheels to confiscate the guns of all who board."

"We're aware of that."

"I realize that in your case this could pose something of a problem Mr. Adams, but I assure you that everyone on this train has been disarmed."

"Do you have any sort of security on this train?" Clint asked.

"Well, of course. We have eight or ten security men on duty at all times."

"And are they armed?"

"Why, yes, of course—"

"And are you armed?"

"I am."

"I assume there are other people onboard who are armed, as well?"

"Well, of course, but we are all authorized—"

"I can't tell you, Mr. Hargrove, how many authorized people have tried to kill me down through the years—and I can't tell you how many people who never would have considered trying while I was armed have tried while I was unarmed."

"I understand your problem, but please, try to understand mine. We have already made allowances for you to bring your horse, which I'm sure will cause a problem or two with people who have had to leave theirs behind. If you are seen carrying a gun—"

"I don't have to be seen," Clint said, interrupting him.

He reached inside his shirt and brought his little .22 Colt New Line. He extended it for Hargrove to examine, and the man did so, spotting something sticking out of the barrel.

"What's this?" he asked, leaning closer. He reached for the barrel with two fingers and extracted what appeared to be a piece of rolled up paper. As he unrolled it the number 100 came into view.

"I see what you mean," the man said, holding the one-hundred-dollar bill in his hand. "I assume then that you will both surrender your sidearms."

"Of course," Hartman said.

"Yes," Clint said reluctantly, tucking the New Line back inside his shirt.

They both removed their gunbelts and handed them to Emerson Hargrove.

"If you don't mind," Clint said, "I'd like mine kept with my horse.'

"Of course. This," Hargrove said, holding up the hundred dollar bill, "was not really necessary."

"Well, good," said Hartman, who had supplied the bill from his winnings of the night before, but as he reached for it, it disappeared inside Hargrove's jacket.

The money tucked away and both gunbelts held in one hand, the man reached behind him and knocked on the door. It was opened and two men stepped out. They were both large, imposing men who wore what appeared to be some sort of uniform and billed caps rather than Stetsons.

"All of our security men are dressed this way so that they are easily recognizable," Hargrove informed them. "It acts as a deterrent."

"I'm sure," Clint said, although he figured that the size of the men and the .45's they wore would act as even more effective deterrents.

He handed one of the men the two gunbelts and said, "Please have these guns held with Mr. Adams' horse in the livestock car."

"Yes, sir."

"Gentlemen," Hargrove said, indicating the open door, "if you will step inside, Hell-on-Wheels is about to get underway."

THIRTEEN

As they entered, they found themselves in a sleeper.

"Certain special guests are accorded special privileges," Hargrove explained, "like a place to sleep."

"And we—" Hartman said.

"Yes," Hargrove said, stopping before a door. "This cabin is for Mr. Adams, and the one right next to it for Mr.—Hartman, is it?"

"That's right."

"You can both go inside and freshen up or get some sleep, if you wish. The next three cars are where the action is, and it goes on continuously."

"Thank you," Clint said.

"If there's anything else I can do to make you comfortable, please let me know."

"Thank you, we will," Hartman said.

As Hargrove started away, he stopped and called out to Clint. "Mr. Adams."

"Yes."

"Mr. Cross asked me to tell you that he is still trying to get that information he promised you. We have a telegraph, so when he has it we will let you know."

"I appreciate that."

"Also, we have not made it general knowledge that you are onboard," Hargrove continued. "If you wish to introduce yourself under another name or use your own, the choice is yours."

"Well," Clint said, "I do appreciate that."

"We are here to serve you," Hargrove said. He turned and walked the length of the car, disappearing through the door at the other end.

"And take our money," Hartman said. "Let's not forget that."

"Let's not."

"Well, it looks as if it sure did me some good to have you for a friend, this time," Hartman said, opening his cabin door and entering.

To his closed door, Clint shouted, "What do you mean, *this* time?"

The cabin was small, but it had a bed, a pitcher of water and a bowl, and a bottle of whiskey. Clint put his saddlebags on the bed, left the whiskey alone, took off his shirt, made use of the pitcher and bowl, and then put on a clean shirt. He checked the New Line, making sure that it was loaded and ready. He felt naked without the modified Colt on his hip, but the New Line against his belly was comforting.

As he stepped out into the hall, Hartman's door opened and he stepped out, also having similarly freshened up.

"Ready for the action?" he asked.

"I'm ready," Clint said.

"You get a bottle of whiskey?" Hartman asked as they walked down the hall.

"I did."

"You drink any?"

"I didn't."

"Suspicious cuss."

"Did you?"

"Hell, no," Hartman said. "I am just as suspicious as you are."

"And just as much of a cuss."

FOURTEEN

"This is it, gents—where the action is."

The man accosted them as soon as they entered the car, and it soon became apparent that he was to Hell-on-Wheels what a barker is to a circus or a Barbary Coast gambling house.

"We've got poker, blackjack, faro, roulette, dice. Name your poison and we can supply it. There's a bar at the other end of the car if you're thirsty, but hurry up and get your piece of luck before she fades away."

They moved past the man and he kept up the patter as if he couldn't stop until he reached the end, regardless of whether anyone was listening.

Everything he said was true, though. There seemed to be a table for every game and not an empty seat in sight.

"I'm afraid the influx of fresh blood has taken up every space," Emerson Hargrove said.

They turned to find him smiling at them—a tall, impeccably dressed man with slicked down hair and a smile that was almost as oily.

"Don't worry, my friends, a space will open up. One

always does. There is space at the bar, however. Would
you allow me to buy you each a drink? Good.''

Placing one hand on the small of each man's back, he
propelled them toward the bar.

"Sam, give these men whatever they want, on me."

The black bartender said, "Yes sir, Mr. Emerson.
What will you gents have?''

"Beer," Clint said.

"Beer," Hartman said. "Cold if you've got it."

"That's the only kind we got," Sam said, staring at him
strangely.

"Sorry," Hartman said, "forgot where I was."

"Let me explain the layout to you gentlemen," Hargrove said. "This is, of course, the gaming car. The next
car is the, uh, relaxation car, shall we call it? It's run by a
lovely lady named Madam Cynthia, otherwise known as
Madam Cyn."

Both men stared at him and Hargrove had the good
grace to look sheepish and say, "Believe me, it wasn't my
idea, but it does seem appropriate."

"Somewhat," Hartman agreed.

"Beyond that we have a special car that you gents
might be interested in."

"And that is?"

"A car for private poker games—high-stakes poker
games, if you get my meaning."

"Not only do we get your meaning," Hartman said,
"but that's what we came here for, Mr. Hargrove."

"Oh, let's not be so formal," Hargrove said. "You can
call me E.G."

"All right, E.G. What do we have to do to get into that
special car?" Clint asked.

"Well, essentially the same thing you have to do
here—wait for a chair to open up. I tell you what, why

don't you look around here for a while and I'll go and see how the games are progressing.''

"Games?"

"Well, of course, there's more than one table—when there are enough players."

"There are always enough players, E.G.," Hartman said.

"I can see you're going to fit in here just fine, Mr. Hartman, just fine."

"Don't be so formal," Hartman said to the man's retreating back, "just call me R.H."

"I guess that makes me C.A."

"Not in my book. Do you see a space at that table?"

"I do," Clint responded.

"What table is it?"

"Blackjack?"

"Not for me," Rick said.

"I'll give it a try," Clint said, leaving his half-finished beer on the bar. Hartman walked behind him, carrying his with him.

"New blood," the dealer said as Clint moved in.

Blackjack was different from poker in that no matter how many people were playing, you were only playing against the house and not against each other.

At that moment there were five people at the table, which was straight on the outside but curved on the inside to allow the dealer to face virtually everyone.

"Chips?"

"One hundred," Clint said, handing over a hundred dollars.

He received ten ten-dollar chips. He promptly bet one and received his first two cards.

"Blackjack," he said, turning over an ace and king of spades."

"You've got this beat," Hartman said in his ear from behind. "I'm going to look around."

"Fine."

The other players all lost and Clint took his payoff and left it on the table. The dealer gave him two cards, a ten and a four, and Clint scraped the table with his cards, asking for another. He received a six and stayed.

When the other players had all received their cards, the dealer turned his over, a ten and a nine, and said, "Nineteen, pay twenty."

"Pay me," Clint said, turning over his cards.

It went that way for a while, with Clint winning more than he lost, and gradually the people at the table began to change.

He was ahead four hundred dollars when the space to his left opened and someone moved into it.

"One hundred dollars in chips, please?" a female voice asked, and he heard the voice and smelled the scent at the same time. He turned to look at her and saw that it was the young blonde from the platform.

Clint was glad to see her there because if she was gambling it meant that she wasn't working the train, and if she wasn't working the train, it meant that she wasn't a whore.

But what was she?

FIFTEEN

Up close, she still looked eighteen, but she had a much prettier face than he had noticed in the dark. Her eyes appeared to be blue, her nose was straight, and her mouth was wide and full. She was wearing a blue dress that buttoned to her neck, and he admired the firm thrust of her breasts. He revised his estimate of her age, placing her in the early twenties, now.

She accepted her chips, looked at him once, and then concentrated on her cards. She played nervously, turning her cards over with convulsive little movements and losing more than she won—while Clint continued to win.

"You want it too badly," he said to her after a while.

"What? I'm sorry, were you speaking to me?" she asked, looking at him wide-eyed.

"Yes, I said you want it too badly."

"Want what?"

"To win?"

"Don't you?"

"Sure, but not like you do."

"Maybe you don't need it as much as I do."

"That might be," he said. "Maybe we can discuss how

81

much you need it over a drink later?''

"I'm sorry, I don't think so."

He smiled and said, "It was just a thought."

"Thank you, but no."

Since there was no limit at the table, you were allowed to bet as much as you wanted to, but Clint noticed that she kept betting twenty dollars at a time.

"Watch," he said to her.

He bet ten dollars, received his cards, bought one, went bust, and flipped his cards in. Next hand he bet twenty.

"What do you mean?"

"When you lose, double your bet," he said.

He received his cards and flipped them over to display another natural blackjack.

"See? You make back what you lost the first time, plus more."

"How many times do you double?"

"As many as you can afford."

She bet ten and then twenty and lost both times. She looked at him nervously and he nodded. She bet forty dollars and flipped her cards over happily to show a natural blackjack.

"I won!" she said breathlessly.

"I saw."

"Thank you."

"You're welcome."

They continued to play and little by little Clint began to lose. Part of the reason was that he was watching the girl more than he was watching his cards. She had begun to win a little, and after an hour he estimated that she was up about fifty dollars. He himself was still ahead, but only by 250 after having been up almost double that.

"Time for a break," he said, cashing in his chips.

"Come back soon, sir," the dealer said.

"To give you a chance to get it back?"

"Of course," the man said, "that's my job."

"Of course," Clint said and left the man ten dollars.

"Thank you, sir."

"I'll cash in," the girl said hurriedly. She turned to Clint and asked, "Does that offer of a drink still hold?"

"It does."

"Then I'd like to take you up on it."

"Fine."

After she received her money, they walked to the bar together.

"This place is not exactly set up for socializing," he said to her.

"That's all right. I don't mind standing at the bar. My name is Wendy Warren, by the way."

"Clint Adams. What will you drink?"

"Do you have sherry?" she asked Sam.

"Yes, ma'am."

"That's what I'll have, please."

"Sir?"

"I'll have a beer."

"Yes, sir."

"So, Wendy," Clint said, "what are you doing on this train?"

"Gambling, just like you," she answered, accepting her drink from Sam.

"No, not just like me," Clint said. "I'm not desperate to win. Oh, I like to win, don't get me wrong, but not desperately—as if I were playing over my head."

"Over your head?"

"With money I couldn't afford to lose."

"And that's what you think I'm doing?" she asked. "Playing with money I can't afford to lose?"

"I think it's obvious. You know, I saw you on the

platform and wondered what you were doing boarding a train like this. Now I know.''

"What do you think you know?'' she asked, raising her chin defiantly.

"I know that you need money and you think this is the way to get it.''

"And it's not?''

"If you win, this is the way to get it,'' he said, ''but it's also the fastest way to lose it.''

"I'll have to take that chance.''

"Why?''

"I don't think I know you well enough to answer that question.''

"I accept that. I can't help wondering, though, how you even found out about this train, let alone qualified to get on it.''

"I don't think I want to answer that, either.''

"Well, what would you like to talk about, then?''

"You?''

"Me?''

"Yes.'' She moved a little closer to him so that her breasts almost touched his arm. "Can you teach me how to gamble better.''

"Better?''

"Well, I know the rudiments of each game, but I'm afraid I'm just not very experienced.''

"I see.''

"You're older and seem to know what you're doing.''

"Well,'' he said, teasing, "I'm not a hell of a lot older.''

"I didn't mean that. I just meant—''

"I know what you meant,'' he said, putting his beer down and becoming serious. "Wendy, it's all right to want to learn how to gamble, but this is the wrong place to do it. As I said, you can lose it all very quickly here."

"That's why I need your help, Clint," she said anxiously. "So I not only won't lose it fast, but so I won't lose it at all."

The desperation was clear in her voice, and as she moved near this time, her breasts did brush his arm—although unintentionally, he was sure.

Staring at her, seeing the pleading look on her face and in her eyes, he thought, well, why the hell not? His entire reason for coming here had been to accompany Rick Hartman and to get a look at Hell-on-Wheels. Of course, while he was here, he intended to gamble, but why not help out Wendy Warren at the same time? Where was the harm in that?

"All right, Wendy. I'll help you."

"Wonderful!" she said excitedly. Her breasts pressed up against him again, harder than before, but he still insisted to himself that it was accidental.

"But you will have to do exactly what I say without question."

"I will."

"At all times."

"I will!"

"That means leaving a table when I say so, even when you're winning."

"I will? Why would I leave a table if I'm winning?" She was honestly puzzled at such a suggestion.

"Because I say so. Understand?"

She stared at him and then said, "Yes, Clint, I understand."

"All right. Now listen," he said and began to explain certain things to her.

SIXTEEN

"Who's your friend?"

Clint looked away from Wendy Warren—who had been listening to him intently for some twenty minutes—and saw Rick Hartman.

"Hello, Rick. How did you do?"

Hartman held up a stack of uncashed chips and Clint figured three hundred.

"You'll never believe what I made it on."

"Surprise me."

"Chess."

"Chess? I didn't even know that you played chess."

"Well, I do, and there's a fella with a table who's playing a hundred dollars a game—and he was doing pretty good, too, until I sat down."

"I would have guessed that there wouldn't be much call for chess on a train like this."

"All kinds of action, isn't that what they promise? I'll bet there's a guy around here playing checkers for money."

"Could be."

"Who's your friend?" Hartman repeated.

"Oh, Rick Hartman meet Wendy Warren."

"I'm pleased to meet you, Miss Warren. Has this lout been bothering you?"

"Oh, no. Clint has been helping me learn to gamble."

"Really?"

"And I wish you'd call me Wendy."

"And you can call me Rick. I didn't know you were giving gambling lessons, Clint."

"I've just been explaining some things to Wendy about odds."

"Has he told you that they're always against you?"

"Yes, but he's also told me that there are times when you can beat them."

"Sure, like when you're incredibly lucky."

"Or when you're good like Clint." Suddenly the young woman yawned and put the back of her hand to her mouth. "Oh, I'm afraid I'm going to have to turn in. Can we continue this tomorrow, Clint. It's fascinating!"

"Sure. Go and get some sleep and I'll see you in the morning."

"For breakfast?"

"For breakfast."

"Good night, then."

"Good night."

"Good night, Rick."

"It was a pleasure meeting you, Wendy."

They both watched her walk through the gaming car and enter the sleeper.

"Guess she's got a cabin," Hartman said. "How does she rate that?"

"That makes her all the more interesting," Clint said. "She wouldn't tell me how she managed to qualify to get on, and now she's even got a cabin."

"I guess she's not a prostitute, after all."

"No, she's no prostitute, but I don't quite know what she is, or if she's for real. She seems too . . . innocent, for want of a better word."

"She's got beautiful eyes," Hartman said, "like chips of blue ice."

"I was thinking the same thing," Clint said, "and a girl with eyes like that . . ."

"I've never heard you use gambling as a means to meet a woman," Hartman said, changing the subject. "She seems to be quite taken with you."

"She's quite taken with what she can learn from me," Clint corrected him.

"You know, you're right," Hartman said, staring down at the other end of the car where it connected with the sleeper. "She is interesting if she managed to get on without knowing how to gamble."

"She says she knows the rudiments of the games, but hasn't had much experience."

"What's her name again?"

"Wendy Warren."

"Warren . . . That name seems familiar to me."

"From where?"

"I don't know, but I'll think of it. Tell me how you did at blackjack."

"I quit while I was ahead."

"Jesus," Hartman said with a look of horror, "what are you trying to do, make money at this?"

SEVENTEEN

"You fellas are in luck," Emerson G. Hargrove's voice said from behind them. They turned to face him and his oily smile.

"A couple of seats in the big game just opened up."

"Good," Hartman said.

"Unfortunately they are at different tables."

"That's all right," Hartman said. "There's no point in having the two best poker players at the same table."

"That's what I like," Hargrove said, "confidence. I should tell you that the game breaks up at five and resumes at noon. Gives people time to freshen up and get some breakfast. It's now two so that gives you three hours of play time."

"Let's not waste it talking, then," Hartman said. "Lead on."

In order to get to the special car, they had to go through Madame Cyn's car, which was an experience in itself.

As you entered the car, you found yourself in a plushly furnished sitting room, and seated on the plush furniture were scantily clad—but tastefully so—women, Madame Cyn's stock. There were blondes, brunettes, redheads,

Chinese, blacks, tall ones, short ones, even a fat one for men with that specialized taste. By the time they walked through the car, prurient interests were somewhat aroused.

"Still want to play poker?" Hargrove asked.

"Let's just say I'm in the mood to make money," Hartman said, "not spend it."

Clint simply nodded.

"Let's go, then."

They exited the pleasure car and entered the special one.

The room was filled with smoke swirling above two densely populated tables. At each table, however, there was an empty seat.

"Gentlemen, I have some fresh blood for you."

There was a general murmur of approval as Clint and Hartman were shown to the empty seats.

"I will let you gentlemen make your own introductions."

"Names don't matter much," said the present dealer at Clint's table, "as long as you bring money."

"I have some," Clint said.

The man looked at him with heavy-lidded eyes—either from fatigue, the smoke, or that's just the way they naturally were.

"Two thousand buys you in, twenty-dollar minimum. You're on your own from there."

It didn't sound particularly steep to Clint until the man said, "No limit on raises."

Most games allowed three raises. No limit on raises is what made it a potentially big game.

"Understand?"

"I understand."

The man started dealing and Clint looked at the other

players in the game, five in all. The names would come as the game went on. He studied their faces to make sure that he knew none of them and then concentrated on the game.

He took the first pot with three kings and continued to win from there, taking every third or fourth hand. He was taking two pots everytime around the table, while the others seem to split evenly.

"You brought a lot of luck with you," one of the other men said.

"Man usually makes his own luck."

Two of the men had been dressed in suits. Their jackets were now on the backs of their chairs. The other three were dressed like Clint, in shirt sleeves, all of which had long since been rolled up. After ten minutes, Clint joined them and rolled his own up.

It had the makings of a very interesting game—if somebody hadn't gone and got killed and ruined it.

EIGHTEEN

Before the man was killed, however, several other things took place.

First, a woman in the gaming car went broke, played for chits, and got in deeper until she couldn't afford to play anymore—and she was then advised of a little known house rule. If you're not playing, then you are taking up the space of someone who could be playing. Therefore, you are required to do something to make up for that lack of income.

In this case, the woman was required to go into Madame Cyn's car and work. She was quite irate about having to do this, but finally agreed. It was fairly obvious that it would not be her first time in such a job.

The second thing that happened was that Emerson G. Hargrove's partner decided that he had taken a liking to one of the women onboard and invited her to his cabin, in spite of a previous agreement with Hargrove to refrain from doing so.

Then, there was a disturbance in the livestock car that required the security man who was stationed outside the Hell-on-Wheels office—which was right next to the cabins of Emerson Hargrove and his partner—to leave his post for fifteen minutes.

That was the third thing that happened.

And the fourth thing that occurred was that Emerson G. Hargrove's partner got killed.

His name was John Rogers.

NINETEEN

Clint had been playing for an hour when Emerson G. Hargrove came back into the car looking disheveled, nervous, and somewhat the worse for wear. Clint could only assume that somebody had gone on a huge winning streak and was in danger of breaking the bank.

He was wrong.

Hargrove spoke to one Mr. Dexter who, the very next time he cut the pot, leaned over Clint's shoulder and said, "Mr. Hargrove would like to speak with you, sir."

"Oh?"

"It's very important. I will take care of your chips, sir."

"Thanks."

"Hey, you're not leaving, are you?" one of the other players said as Clint stood up.

Because Mr. Dexter had spoken barely above a whisper so that only Clint could hear him, Clint decided that Mr. Hargrove wanted to see him in private with little or no fanfare.

"Got to answer a call of nature," he said. "I'll be right back."

He walked to the door of the car, opened it, and stepped out in the alcove that all the cars seemed to have between the inner and outer doors. He found Emerson Hargrove waiting there for him, mopping his brow with an already sopping handkerchief. Clint found that odd because after being in the special car for an hour he found the alcove quite cool.

"You want to see me?"

"Yes, Mr. Adams. Uh, something . . . untoward has happened."

"Untoward?"

"Difficult to handle."

"You have a security force, Mr. Hargrove. Why bring it up to me?"

"It is something we are not set up to handle, Mr. Adams. I would dearly love your assistance in the matter."

"I don't understand."

"Would you come with me, please? I can m–make it clearer to you by showing you."

"All right," Clint said in a resigned tone, "lead the way."

Hargrove led him through the pleasure car, the gaming car, and the livestock car to another car that apparently housed the headquarters of Hell-on-Wheels.

"This is where our office and our cabins are, as well as our safe."

"Ah," Clint said, thinking he'd discovered the problem, "has your safe been hit?"

"Would that that were the problem," Hargrove said, mopping his brow again. "This way, please."

He led Clint to the closed door of a cabin and nervously knocked on it. The door was opened by one of his security force, who nodded and stepped aside to allow them entry.

As Clint entered behind Hargrove, he saw what the problem was. There was a man lying on the floor bleeding from a small head wound.

"Dead?" he asked.

"Quite."

Clint leaned over to examine the body. The wound on the head was the only one he could see and was apparently caused by a small caliber bullet. There was no exit wound, which meant the bullet was still somewhere inside the body. Small slugs had a habit of traveling inside the body instead of bursting out the other side, and it would not have been unusual for this bullet to have lodged in the dead man's leg or foot.

"Who did it?"

"I'm afraid we have no idea," Hargrove said. "My man found him this way and called it to my attention. This is terrible!"

"It's even worse for him," Clint said. "Who is he?"

"He's my partner."

"I see. Well, Mr. Hargrove, you certainly have a situation here, but what can I do for you?"

"You are a famous former lawman, sir. You can find out who did it."

"That's for the law to find out. Just pull into the next town and hand it over to them."

"I'm afraid it's not that simple. If I bring the law into this, it would mean the end of everything."

"I'm sure your partner is beyond worrying about that now."

"Of course, but there are certain . . . eastern interests to be protected. If I allowed this problem to be discovered before we knew who did it, my life—my livelihood would be in danger."

"Let me get this straight. You want me to find out who

did this so that when you do turn it over to the law you can give them the killer as well?''

''That's it exactly.''

''That's asking a lot, Mr. Hargrove. I'm not a detective, you know.''

''I know your reputation quite well, Mr. Adams. I am confident that you can clear this matter up for us.''

''I don't know—''

''Please!'' Hargrove said with more than a little desperation in his voice.

''I'd have to think about it.''

''What shall I do with Mr. Rogers, sir?'' the security man asked.

Clint started at the sound of the dead man's name.

''Rogers. Your partner's name is Rogers?''

''Yes,'' Hargrove said, ''John Rogers. Why?''

John Rogers was the name of the man Delilah Madison had wanted to hire him to kill.

Suddenly, he had an interest in finding John Rogers' killer.

TWENTY

"Why are you getting yourself involved in this?" Rick Hartman asked.

"Because Hargrove asked me nicely."

"Why are you getting me involved in this? I could be playing poker."

"Relax. It's almost time for the game to break up."

"I could make a lot of money in an hour."

"I need your help."

"I don't understand this."

"Then let me explain it to you before the others get here," Clint said. *Here* was the office of Emerson Hargrove and his late partner, where Clint had set up shop after examining the body a little more thoroughly. When he had finished that, he had asked Hargrove if there was a place they could put the body so it wouldn't start to smell.

"We've got a car farther back with some ice. We can put him in there."

And that's what they had done. After the body was moved, Clint moved into the office, and Hargrove went to get the security man who should have been on guard in the hallway.

"Remember I told you that Delilah wanted to hire me to kill a man?"

"Sure. You turned her down. So what?"

"That man's name was John Rogers."

"So?"

"The dead man's name is John Rogers."

"So wh—wait a minute." Hartman thought it over a minute and then said hopefully, "There could be two John Rogers, you know."

"I don't believe in coincidence, Rick, and neither do you."

"Sure I do," Hartman said lamely.

"Never mind."

"Well, I still don't see why you have to get involved. Why don't they just turn it over to the law in the next town?"

Patiently, Clint explained Hargrove's reasoning for not doing that.

"The end of Hell-on-Wheels," Hartman mused aloud. "I guess I can understand his concern—especially if he would be the one held responsible for it."

"Who else would there be? His partner's dead?"

"Well, they could hold the killer responsible."

"That's not the way the world works, Rick."

"I know. Well, what are you going to do first?"

"Find out what John Rogers was doing tonight and who with."

"What about Delilah Madison? Do you think she finally found somebody to take the job?"

"I don't know, but if she didn't, then we're dealing with coincidence here, and you know what I think about that."

"Then you think you're looking for somebody who planned this, not a random killer."

"That's the assumption I'm going to go on—based on my experience with Delilah."

"What do you think Rogers did to make her want him dead so badly?"

"I don't know, and we may never know, but it's not important. All I need to do is find the killer and have him implicate her. The reasons can come out in court."

"You really think you're going to find him?"

"I've been lucky once or twice before," Clint said. "Why not again?"

"Why not?"

There was a knock on the door then and Clint nodded at Hartman who opened the door.

Emerson Hargrove entered and brought with him one of his security men.

"This is the man who was supposed to be on duty out in this hall."

"All right. Why don't you leave us alone?"

Hargrove nodded, glared at the man as if it were his fault, and then left. Like most of the others, this one was tall and heavyset, almost fat around the middle. He had gray hair at his temples and in his beard stubble and appeared to be in his forties. He looked for all the world like a punched-out heavyweight.

"What's your name?"

"Sid Borden."

"Can I call you Sid?"

"Yes, sir."

"Cut out the sir. What's your background for this kind of work, Sid?"

"Five years with Pinkerton."

"Quit?"

The man fidgeted and then said, "I got fired."

"What for?"

"Drinking."

"Are you still drinking?"

"No, sir."

"So you weren't off somewhere taking a nip?"

"No, sir."

"You ever box?"

The man's face took on animation for the first time and he said, "Yes, sir, before I was with the Pinks."

"Were you any good?"

"I was all right. I was in line for a title shot, but . . . but I drank that away, too."

"Not drinking anymore, though, right?"

"That's right, sir. I swear it. I haven't had a drop since I left the Pinks."

"All right. What's your regular job, Sid?"

"I guard the office—make sure nobody goes in and tries to rob it."

"That means you're out in the hall all the time."

"Yes."

"Which means that you're also guarding the cabins of Mr. Hargrove and Mr. Rogers."

"I can see their cabins, but I'm guarding the office." Borden apparently wanted to make that very clear.

"What happened tonight, Sid?"

"Well, every so often I peeked my head in the office for a few seconds, just to check it out. One time, when I came out into the hall, I saw Mr. Rogers and a girl sneaking into his cabin."

"Why would he have to do that, Sid? Sneak in, I mean. Isn't he the boss?"

"He and Mr. Hargrove, yeah."

"Why sneak in, then?"

The guard shifted from one foot to the other without answering and Clint thought he knew why.

"I can understand your loyalty to your employers, but one of them is dead. I need your help to find out how and why . . . and who."

"Yeah, all right," Borden said. "Mr. Rogers had a habit of picking out some girl from the crowd and taking her into his cabin. Sometimes it don't matter if she's married or not, if you get my meaning."

"I do. Go on."

"Well, that was probably why Mr. Rogers felt he had to sneak into his room so I wouldn't see. See, he promised Mr. Hargrove he wouldn't do it anymore."

"A promise he obviously had no intention of keeping."

"He wasn't a bad guy, Mr. Rogers, he just really liked the ladies, you know? I think when he made the promise he really wanted to keep it, but he just can't say no to a woman . . . if she's willing, I mean."

"I understand. Did you get a good look at the woman, Sid?"

"No, sir."

"Not even when she left?"

"That's just it. I never saw her leave."

"How did she get out, then?"

"Well, I can hear everything that goes on in the livestock car because it's the next one. I heard some commotion in there—"

"What kind of commotion?"

"Shouting, banging, horses whinnying, like that."

"And you went to see what it was?"

"Yes, sir."

"And what was it?"

"Well, apparently a lantern had fallen and started a small fire. I got there in time to help Jack put it out."

"Were any of the animals hurt."

"No, sir." For the second time the man's face looked

animated. "I know you got that big black in there, sir, and—well, he is just fine. He just stood there calm while the other horses panicked. That's quite an animal."

"Thanks. I'm pretty proud of him. What happened after you came back, Sid?"

"Well, I took up my post like always, checked the office once or twice, but kept an eye on the hallway."

"Why did you do that, Sid? I mean, I assume that means you didn't go all the way into the office and could see the hallway at all times."

"That's right."

"Why did you change your routine?"

"I wanted to be able to tell Mr. Hargrove when the girl went in and when she came out."

"But you never saw her leave."

"No. After a while I got a little worried."

"What about?"

"I was afraid Mr. Rogers might have fallen asleep. I didn't want Mr. Hargrove to catch him with the girl in there and all."

"But why? You were going to tell him about it, anyway, weren't you?"

The man lowered his head and then said, "Only if he asked."

"I see. Have you covered for Mr. Rogers before?"

"A few times."

"For money?"

"No, sir. He's the one who gave me this job when nobody else would touch me. I owed him."

"So when you got worried what did you do?"

"I knocked on the door and there wasn't any answer."

"Then what?"

"I opened it."

"With a key?"

"No, sir. I have a key to the cabins, but I didn't need it. It was unlocked."

"And you found Mr. Rogers?"

"Yes, sir. On the floor."

"You knew he was dead?"

"Oh, yes, sir. I've seen dead men before. I went and got Mr. Hargrove after that, and then he told me to stay there while he got some help."

Meaning me, Clint thought. Had Hargrove thought of sending for the Gunsmith right away? That was a question worth asking.

"All right, Sid, I guess that's all."

"I guess I'm gonna lose my job over this, huh?"

"Not if I can help it. You did your job as far as I can see and maybe saved the train from having a major fire."

"Thank you, sir."

"By the way, Sid, how did the lantern in the livestock car fall?"

"Now that's the damndest thing. Jack says he knew he had it secure enough because the same thing happened to him once before and he wanted to make sure it never happened again."

"Where was the lamp?"

"On the wall just inside the door."

"So somebody would have been able to reach in and knock it down?"

"Very easily."

Clint thought it over and then decided he had no more questions—not for Sid Borden, anyway.

"All right. Just go outside and take up your regular post. There's a possibility I may need you."

"I'll be here, sir. Thank you."

After Borden left, Hartman looked at Clint and said, "You make my head spin."

"Why?"

"All those questions. You're really taking this thing seriously. How do you come up with them all?"

"I told you, I've been lucky once or twice before."

"Aren't you the man who always says that a man makes his own luck?"

"Yeah," Clint admitted, "I guess I am."

"All right, then, what's next? If I'm going to be your assistant, I want to do more than stand around and listen to you interrogate people."

"Fine. Why don't you go and talk to Jack in the livestock car and see what he has to say? I'm going to talk to a few more security people."

"All right. Can I grill him the way you did the security man?"

"Just ask him some questions, Rick. Don't get carried away."

"If I'm not going to get to play cards," he grumbled while going out the door, "the least you can do is let me get carried away."

TWENTY-ONE

Clint questioned several of the other security men as to what they might have seen or heard, but none of them had anything to add to what Borden had said.

Hartman returned from questioning Jack—whose last name was Forrest—and the man from the livestock car said pretty much what Borden had, that it was possible that someone had knocked over the lantern.

After that, Hartman took a seat again while Clint questioned Emerson G. Hargrove.

"Don't be so nervous, E.G.," Clint said, trying to soothe the man.

"Oh, can the E.G. crap," Hargrove said. "That's for the suckers. My real name is Ernie, Ernie Hargrove."

"Why the E.G.?" Hartman asked.

"It sounds like P.T. You know, P.T. Barnum?"

"Makes sense to me," Hartman said, studying the ceiling.

"All right, Ernie," Clint said, "tell me about John Rogers."

"What do you want to know?"

"Everything, anything. Just start talking."

"Well, he was a good partner except for one thing. He couldn't keep his hand off women. Pretty women, ugly women, single women, married women, if they were willing he was attracted to them, and he did something about it."

"You know he had a woman in there with him tonight, don't you?"

"Yeah, Borden told me. You don't think I should fire the man?"

"No, Ernie. He probably saved your train by putting out the fire when he did."

"Yeah, I guess."

"What else about Rogers?"

"He had a head for business. This whole thing was his idea; he handled the money and the books. My part was to handle the suckers."

"I'm getting tired of being called that," Hartman said.

"No offense," Hargrove assured him.

"Keep talking."

"He had highfalutin tastes."

"What do you mean?"

"He ate funny. He liked to eat snails and fish eggs."

"Escargot and cavier?" Hartman asked.

"That's it, and champagne, even if it was warm. He said champagne tasted rich, even when it wasn't cold."

"What else?"

"He dressed fine, real fine. Wouldn't even leave his cabin unless every hair was in place and every button was buttoned."

It went on like that for twenty minutes, Ernie Hargrove telling everything he knew about the deceased John Rogers.

"Did I say he liked women?"

"Yes."

"Whores? Did I say that?"

"No."

"Well, he did. Whores, saloon girls—"

"Saloon owners?" Clint asked.

"If they was women."

"You ever hear of a woman named Delilah Madison?"

"No, but if she was one of John's women I never wanted to know their names."

"What about you, Ernie?"

"What about me?"

"Did you get along with Rogers?"

"We got along fine."

"I heard that you argued, especially about his women."

"I'm gonna fire that Borden."

"You do and I'll leave this whole thing in your lap."

"All right, all right. Yeah, so we argued about his women. I didn't mind if he took a whore or two, but when he started taking the suckers'—uh, I mean the customers' women, their wives . . . He should have drawn the line somewhere!"

"Yeah," Clint said, "I guess he should have. That's all, Ernie. Go get a drink and come back in fifteen minutes."

"Yeah, sure. You fellas want anything?"

"Yes, bring us back a couple of beers."

"Cold," Hartman said.

Hargrove frowned and said, "That's the only kind we got."

"Sorry."

After Hargrove was gone, Hartman looked at Clint and said, "So?"

"So what?"

"Who killed him?"

"All I know is that it was a woman. She may have had an accomplice—male or female—but I feel certain he was killed by a woman."

"Why?"

"Because he had a woman in his cabin."

"So what? She could have let her male accomplice into the room."

"She could have."

"But you don't think so."

"No."

"Okay, tell me what you think?" Clint asked.

"I think her accomplice knocked over that lamp to start the fire and draw Borden away from the hall," Rick said.

"And then she could have let him in."

"Why would Rogers have answered the door?"

"She answered it."

"No, a womanizer like Rogers would have had her in bed by then. It's faster if she kills him because she doesn't have to think of an excuse to get out of bed, answer the door, and let a man in. Remember, Borden wasn't gone that long. Besides, they were both naked when she killed him."

"Jesus, how do you figure that?" Hartman said.

"You heard what Ernie said. Rogers wouldn't leave his room without buttoning all his buttons."

"So."

"So I examined the body. His shirt was buttoned wrong. The top button was in the second buttonhole, and so on down the line. That's the sort of thing a woman would have done if she were dressing a dead man fast."

"You noticed that?"

"Yes. Also, there was no blood on the outside of his collar, only on the inside. She put the shirt on him after she shot him and put it on over the blood."

"You noticed that, too, huh? I'm starting to get impressed," Hartman said sincerely.

"Don't be. They're just logical observations."

"So she dressed him so that he wouldn't be found naked because that might have given the killer away as a woman."

"Right."

"And in dressing him, she gave herself away."

"Right again."

"Okay, hot shot, then who is she?"

"That I don't know," Clint said. Then he added, "Yet."

Hargrove returned precisely twenty minutes later with two cold beers.

"Thanks, Ernie. Sit down."

"What? More about John?"

"No, I've heard enough about John. Tell me of anything unusual involving a woman that has happened on this trip."

"Unusual. When you're dealing with women everything is unusual—"

"Spare me that stuff, Ernie, and answer the question."

"Naw, nothing unusual—wait a minute."

"Something?"

"Yeah, we had a woman who tapped out and John told her that since she was taking up the space of a paying customer, she was going to have to earn her way."

"Doing what?"

"Working in Madam Cyn's car."

"He turned her into a prostitute because she tapped out?" Clint asked. "Hell of a nice guy you got for a partner, Ernie."

"It wasn't nothing. The girl's worked before."

"Can you bring her here. I want to talk to her."

"Sure." Ernie leaned forward and said, "You figure a woman done John in?"

"That's what I figure, Ernie, and I also figure that whoever she is she was hired by another woman."

"What makes you figure that?"

"Because a woman tried to hire me to kill him."

"You?"

"Back in Omaha."

"That one you were asking me about?"

"That's the one. Go and get the woman, Ernie, huh? I'd like to wrap this up and get some gambling in."

"I'll bring her, all right," Hargrove said, standing up. "Me and a couple of my boys."

"I think you can handle a woman yourself, Ernie. Besides, taking a couple of your musclemen along would attract attention. You don't want to attract attention, do you?"

"Jesus, no."

"And just ask her nicely to come. I said a woman may have killed John, not this woman."

"What if she doesn't want to come?"

"Tell her you figured out a way for her to pay her way without working as a whore. She'll come then."

"Right," Ernie said and left.'

"You think he'll try and drag her here by her hair?" Rick asked.

"If anything, she'll drag him here by his hair. I never knew a woman who wouldn't jump at the chance to get out of whoring."

TWENTY-TWO

The woman's name was Fay Gardner. She had a full
body, dark hair, and a quick tongue. She appeared to be in
her early thirties, and there was a hard, brittle look to her
that almost kept her from being attractive.

Almost.

"All right, Mr. Hargrove," Clint said. "You can leave
her here."

"Sure."

She followed Hargrove's progress out the door, and
then she turned to Clint with her hands on her hips,
brazenly meeting his eyes.

"He jump to your tune?"

"Not really. Actually, I work for him."

"You could have fooled me."

"All right, have it your way. I'm doing him a favor."

"Favors don't come cheap. I should know. Am I gonna
have to do you the rest of the way? Is that how I earn my
keep?"

"You earn your keep, Fay, by answering a few questions."

"That's all?"

"That's all."

She looked at Hartman and said, "Seems too easy.

Hartman shrugged.

"Doesn't he talk?"

"He's a deaf-mute."

"Hey, yeah? But he heard me."

"He reads lips."

"Really? That's crazy."

"Fay, who put you in Madam Cyn's car to work?"

"Who put me? You people put me."

"Not me."

"No, not you. The guy who just left, his partner put m
in. What's his name?"

"Rogers. John Rogers."

"That's the man. He said I had to earn my way 'caus
was taking up space."

"Well, don't worry. If you answer my questions y
won't have to go back to Madam Cyn's."

"Hey, really?"

"Really."

"Maybe I'll stay with you the rest of the way, anywa
How about that?"

"We'll talk about it. First, answer my questions."

"Whatever you say, handsome."

"Did you kill John Rogers tonight?"

"What? Say that again."

"I said did you kill—"

"I heard you! What kind of question is that? Someo
killed that bastard?"

"A woman, Fay," Clint said. "A woman killed hi
Was it you?"

"Hell, no, it wasn't me. I wouldn't have had the ner
to kill him, although I wish I had. You know why he rea
put me in Madam Cyn's car?"

"Because he said you had to spend the rest of the trip with him to pay your way and you refused."

"How did you know that?" she asked, staring at him in awe.

"He keeps doing things like that," Hartman said.

She looked at him and said, "I thought you was deaf and dumb."

"Dumb? Who said dumb? Nobody said dumb. Deaf-mute was the phrase that was used."

"But you ain't."

Hartman stared at her in surprise, touched his ears and mouth, and said, "A miracle!"

"Hold it, Rick," Clint said. "All right, Fay. Can you prove you didn't kill him?"

"Sure, I been working, remember. In no time at all I became Madam Cyn's best girl. Everybody wants to climb on the gal that's got to work off her losses."

"So you've been busy."

"I'm so sore I couldn't lay down for you if I wanted to—well, in your case I'd make an exception."

"You didn't go to Rogers' room with him earlier tonight? Say a couple of hours ago?"

"Never in a million years, friend. I'd almost rather have sex with anyone other than that dude. He just gave me the creeps. He thought I couldn't turn him down, you know. Boy, was he surprised when I did."

"All right, Fay. You can go."

"Where? I can't gamble and I ain't going back to whoring. Where do I go?"

"Give her your key, Rick."

"*My* key?"

Clint nodded.

Rick took out his key and tossed it to her. She caught it in one hand.

"Thanks. Try to be quiet when you come in, will ya? I'll be tryin' to get some sleep."

"I'll take off my boots first."

"Thanks. And you, handsome, I owe you one for getting me out of that car. I won't forget."

"Just get some sleep, Fay," Clint told her. "You don't owe me a thing."

"Says you," she said and left.

"Why my key?"

"You heard her," Clint said, "she wouldn't have been able to help herself if she was in my cabin with me. By putting her in with you, we remove any temptation from her path and she can rest."

Hartman stared at him for a few seconds and then said, "If I wasn't so interested in watching you work, I'd take a poke at you."

"Save your poke for Fay."

TWENTY-THREE

After Clint did all he could do from the office, he got out and decided to walk around. One of the things he wanted to do was talk to Madam Cynthia and find out if she backed up Fay's story, but first he wanted to stop at the bar in the gaming car.

He walked through the car with Hartman and Hargrove in tow, Hargrove trotting to keep up with them and speaking in low, urgent tones.

"Do you know who did it?"

"Not yet, Ernie."

"Will you know before we reach the next town?"

"Which is?"

"North Platte."

"That's still Nebraska."

"We won't get to Wyoming for a couple of days."

"How long before we reach North Platte."

"Midnight tonight."

"Tonight?" Clint asked, sidling up to the bar. He turned to face Hargrove and said, "You want me to solve this thing by tonight?"

Hargrove nodded and said, "We could hand the killer

over in North Platte and be on our way. Can you do it?''

Clint stared at Hargrove for a few moments, exchanged glances with Hartman, and then said—to everyone's surprise, including his own—''Yeah, I probably can.''

''Wonderful! Sam,'' Hargrove said after they had ordered their drinks, ''from now on anything Mr. Adams wants—''

''And Mr. Hartman,'' Clint said.

''Yes, anything either one of these gentlemen wants is complimentary, understand?''

''Yes, sir, I understand. I know what complimentary means. Anything these two gents want is free.''

Clint said to Hartman, ''Who on this train knows all that's going on?''

Without hesitation Hartman said, ''The bartender, of course.''

''Why don't you see what Sam has to say while I go and talk to Madam Cynthia?''

''Sure you wouldn't want to switch jobs?''

''I'm sure.''

''What a division of labor,'' Hartman said, shaking his head.

''What about me?'' Hargrove asked.

''Ernie, why don't you go and relax somewhere. Everything on your train is still running smoothly. The suckers are still losing their money. Just take it easy, okay?''

''Take it easy,'' Hargrove repeated. ''How am I supposed to do that? What if the madman—or woman—who killed poor John wants to kill me next?''

''I don't think there's any danger of that,'' Rick Hartman said, ''unless you've been holding out on us.''

''Naw, not me,'' Hargrove said.

''Have you gotten any women mad enough to kill you, Ernie?'' Hartman asked.

"Not me," Hargrove said earnestly. "I got respect for women."

"Then according to Clint's theory, you're safe."

And then, contradicting the statement he'd just made, Ernie said, "Besides, they're more trouble than they're worth."

"Sometimes I agree with you, Ernie," Clint said, "and then again, sometimes I don't."

After Ernie Hargrove had staggered away, Hartman said to Clint, "Why did you tell him you'd have it wrapped up by tonight?"

"Why make him feel more pressure than he already does? He's about to cave in, as it is. Besides, I think I might just be able to do it by tonight, and then we can get back to the business at hand."

"Gambling."

"What else is there?"

As Clint started away, Hartman grabbed his arm and said, "You going in there now?" He meant the pleasure car.

"Sure. It's my duty."

"Well, if you're not out in . . . a couple hours, I'll come in and get you."

Patting his friend's hand, Clint said, "You don't know what a comfort that is to me, Rick."

TWENTY-FOUR

The killer opened the door and let herself into the cabin. She looked around and then decided to use the bed while she waited. She didn't think the man would mind, especially if she were naked when she got there. She found that a man would forgive her almost anything if she were naked.

Undressing and sliding between the sheets—maybe she'd even get some sleep while she was waiting—she told herself that she was dealing with a very clever man here, a man who was dangerous.

Luckily, she herself was clever or she wouldn't have lasted three years in the business of killing people, but the Gunsmith had lasted a lot longer than that in a similar business—the business of constantly being a target for people who wanted to kill him.

The outcome, she thought as she drifted off to sleep, should be extremely interesting.

TWENTY-FIVE

As Clint entered the car alone, he was immediately assailed by two women, both wearing diaphanous wrappers that barely hid their charms, which were in both cases considerable. Behind them, about eight other women sat on overstuffed divans and chairs. Some were already occupied with customers; others waited patiently.

Patience was apparently a virtue these two women did not possess.

Both women were as aggressive as they were buxom. Both were also fairly competitive, and it took the appearance of a somewhat older, handsome—if a little plump—woman to extricate Clint from their clutches.

"I can save you from this, if you like," the older woman said.

"Please. They're making a choice almost impossible to make."

"Girls, give the man room to breathe."

"Don't forget my name," one of the women said, stroking his cheek.

"Or mine," the other said, stroking him in a somewhat more intimate place.

He had already forgotten both.

"You have to try to get those two to overcome their shyness," Clint said to the woman.

"I'll work on it. Would you like someone along somewhat sleeker lines? We have Gloria—over there by the divan. She's long, limber, and in addition she's got that lovely cocoa skin."

Clint looked at the woman in question, a tall, black girl with long, slender legs, small breasts, high cheekbones, and full lips.

"She's straight off the boat from Africa."

"More than likely she's straight off the train from San Francisco," Clint said, and the woman gave him a long, studied look.

"Actually," he said, "I think I'd prefer something along more . . . mature lines."

"I see," the woman said, studying him even closer. She was clearly in her early forties, not as spry as she once had been. Her body was showing signs of age—a thickening in the waist, with an overblown effect in the full bosom—and there was some gray in her brown hair, but he had no doubt that she would still be extremely desirable to some men.

"Would you like to come to my office?"

"Why not?"

She led the way to a small cabin that was barely large enough for the two of them and a small wooden desk.

"What's on your mind?"

"Why should anything—"

"I'm not bad to look at, and I'm real good in bed still, but when a man says he might prefer me over one of my younger girls, I start to get suspicious. I'm sorry, but that's the way I am. Tell me I'm wrong. Tell me all you want is some experience, and we'll set a price."

"Okay, you're right. I do want something slse."

"I thought as much. What can I do for you?"

"I'm doing a little job for the owners of the train."

With a look of intense distaste, she said, "If you mean Rogers and that little weasel Hargrove, they're just the managers."

Clint decided very quickly how he wanted to play it and said, "No, Madam Cynthia, I'm talking about the owners back East."

That made the woman stand up a little straighter and she said, "I'm sending their share in regular. What more do they want?"

"I think they're concerned over the quality of your girls."

"My girls are high class. So some of them are a little aggressive. Some men like that—"

"I think your stock is questionable when you take on a customer just because she can't pay her way."

"Oh, that!" she said as if it were a great relief. "That was Rogers' idea, and I got to tell you it was probably one of his best. The girl was a natural, and if you really wanted something more mature, she'd be the one I'd give you."

"Then she worked out?"

"She not only worked out, but I'd like to have her as a regular. As a matter of fact, she disappeared a little while ago. You wouldn't know anything about that, would you?"

"I would. She won't be coming back."

"Something happen to her?"

"Management decided they made a mistake."

"That figures. The best move they've ever made and they take her back. Don't tell me she went and gave into that sleaze Rogers?"

"No, I sprang her."

"For yourself?"

''For herself. There's no reason to make her work just because she tapped out. That's not the way the owners want their customers treated.''

''Well, you tell her I'll pay her to come back, and she can pick and choose her customers. That girl is a professional, and I need more like her.''

''I see. Has she been working in this car ever since she was put in here?''

''She's been busy, I'll tell you that.''

''No time for a break, or perhaps a visit to one of the private cabins?''

''No, she's been here. Why?''

He smiled and said, ''Maybe we'll hire her for you.''

''You don't understand, Mr.—''

''Adams.''

''Mr. Adams, I do my own hiring.''

''I see. Well, I'll tell her you're interested.''

''You do that,'' she said, eyeing him suspiciously now. ''Is there anything else we can do for you?''

''No, I prefer not to, uh, pay—''

''Since you're working for the owners, you wouldn't have to. I could send you Gloria in your cabin or you could make another choice.''

''It's very tempting, but I think I'm going to have to get some sleep now.''

''You let me know when.''

He turned to leave, then stopped short, and turned back to her. ''Do you supply Rogers and Hargrove with girls, too?''

She made a face and said, ''Upon demand. Rogers all the time, Hargrove every once in a while.''

''And the girls do whatever you tell them? Go to whoever you send them to without question?''

''They have minds of their own, but in the end I win

out—if they want to keep their jobs.''

"I see. You didn't happen to send anyone to Mr. Rogers' cabin tonight, did you?''

"No, not tonight,'' she said. "Hey, what the hell is going on?''

"Not a thing, really. I'm just nosy. Good night, Madam Cynthia.''

"Drop the Madam stuff and just call me Cynthia. You tell me when you're ready for one of my girls—or when you're ready to tell me the truth.''

"I'll let you know, Cynthia,'' he said, "on both counts.''

TWENTY-SIX

When Clint walked back through the sitting room portion of the cabin, he saw that many of the women had disappeared—including long, lithe Gloria and the aggressive duo. There was one woman left, and she was apparently negotiating with a man.

When he reentered the gaming car, he found Hartman nursing a drink at the bar. Sam was gone from behind the bar. The disadvantage of not having a private cabin became immediately clear because every available space had been claimed by one sucker—customer—or another for sleep, and there were people sprawled everywhere. Clint even spotted several women among the clutter.

"Looks like a bomb hit."

"Curfew," Hartman said. "Whoever can't afford a private cabin or a night—or morning—with one of Madam Cynthia's girls just picks a spot and plops down."

"Well, that's what I'm going to do. Pick a spot in my cabin and plop down."

Hartman put his glass down and walked with Clint down the length of the car, stepping over a body or a limb here and there along the way.

"What did you find out?"

"Madam Cynthia says that Fay is a pro and didn't leave the car until Ernie got her."

"But she is a pro."

"Yes."

"So it couldn't have taken much, or been much of a hardship, for her to be working there."

Clint frowned and said, "It would be a hardship if she didn't want to be there. Some people are good at what they do even if they don't want to do it. Some people just can't help but be good."

"You have a point."

"What did you get from Sam?"

"Idle gossip about his bosses. He felt they were getting along less and less each day and that they were eventually coming to a parting of the ways."

"He doesn't know that Rogers is dead?"

"No. What about Madam Cyn?"

"I didn't tell her and she didn't appear to know. She's curious, though, and figures that something is going on. She'll have to be told eventually."

"Leave that up to Ernie."

"I've got more questions for him, and I can probably get our guns back now that we're investigating a murder, but all of that can wait until after we've gotten some sleep."

At Hartman's cabin they stopped and he asked Clint, "How were you doing in that game?"

"I was winning. There was only one other good player at the table."

"Eventually we might get to sit at one table, and it could get interesting—if we ever get to play again, that is."

"You can play later today. I'll try to muddle through

without you. After all, that's what you came here to do.''

''You sure?''

''Positive. Don't worry, if I need you I'll give a yell.''

''And I'll come running.''

''Deal. Get some sleep.''

Hartman reached for his key and then remembered he didn't have it.

''I hope my guest didn't lock me out.''

He reached for the door and found it unlocked.

''Oh, speaking of your guest . . .''

''Yeah?''

Clint grinned and said, ''If you need me, give a yell.''

TWENTY-SEVEN

When Clint entered his cabin, he became aware of another presence, and his hand drifted to the New Line, but the smell in the air told him he wouldn't need it. He recognized the perfume scent.

"Wendy?" he said into the darkness.

"Oh, shoot," her voice came back. She was nearest the lamp and turned it up. She was sitting up in his bed, naked, her pale breasts given a slightly yellowish tinge by the glow of the lamp. They were small, but appeared very firm and round. Her aureola were wide, and the nipples at the center were already stiff and hard.

"I really wanted to surprise you when you slid into bed, Clint," she said, looking disappointed.

"Wendy, what are you doing here?"

"You can't expect me to sleep in the gaming car with the rest of the cattle, and Madam Cyn's car holds little appeal for me."

"You mean you don't have a cabin?"

"I just thought I'd share yours."

Her eyes were guileless, but he thought this a pretty bold move on the part of a girl who had seemed so innocent and naive earlier in the evening.

"I know you think me bold," she said as if reading his mind, "but you impressed me last night. You were nice to me, agreeing to help me, and I wanted to . . . to repay your kindness somehow."

"This isn't necessary."

"This is the way I want to do it, though. Also, I needed a place to sleep and . . . I find you attractive."

"I'm flattered, but—"

"Don't you find me attractive? Desirable?"

"All of that," he said and then added, "and you're very young."

"I'm not so young," she said. "I'm twenty-one."

"That's young."

"It's old enough to work in Madam Cyn's. Old enough to gamble. And it's old enough to know what I want." She extended her arms to him and said, "I want you. Come on, Clint, it's very warm in here."

Jesus Christ, he thought, feeling his cock stiffen and swell.

She pulled the sheet up to her neck and said, "Come and get warm."

After about five minutes, Hartman finally made up his mind and decided to slip into bed beside the sleeping Fay. It was, after all, his cabin. If she didn't like it, she could sleep on the floor.

He usually slept naked, but in deference to his guest, he went to bed wearing his underwear. He pulled the sheet aside without turning up the lamp and got into bed, becoming immediately aware as he did of the heat her body was radiating. Why were women just naturally so much hotter than men?

He tried to get comfortable without waking her, and as his arm accidentally brushed her, he realized with a start that she was naked.

Christ, he thought, as his penis began to swell involuntarily.

She stirred and rolled over, bringing her hip into contact with his. Then her hand drifted over and settled on his crotch. With a quick little movement, her hand darted inside his underwear, holding him loosely.

"Mmm, are you glad to see me?" she asked, stroking him with a gentle touch.

"Fay—"

"I was wondering when you'd get here," she said, squeezing him tighter. "I thought maybe you'd gone to Madam Cyn's."

"The thought had occurred to me," he said, trying to hold back a groan.

She thumbed the swollen head of his penis and said, "I can give you anything you could have gotten there and more—and for free."

"Fay—"

"You don't want it?" she asked, using her other hand to slide his underwear down.

"Uh—" he said, closing his eyes. His penis pulsed madly in her hand.

"Sure you do," she said.

She slid her head beneath the sheet; then, her mouth and tongue moved wetly over his belly. She took off his underwear and discarded them and then cupped his balls with her other hand. He settled onto his back, waiting, and suddenly her tongue was on him, licking him up and down. He waited for her mouth and it came, settling down around him, suckling him into its warmth. Her hands slid beneath him and clutched his ass tightly, digging into him with her nails. He moaned and reached for her head . . .

"I was afraid you might have gone to Madam Cyn's," Wendy said as Clint got into bed with her. She was right. It was very warm, and her skin was burning.

"I don't ever pay for my pleasure, Wendy."

"I'm glad," she said, moving her hands over his chest and down across his belly. When she encountered his penis, she caught her breath. "God, you're big. I've never felt one so big."

"Your experience must be limited," he said.

"Don't make fun," she said. "There's a lot you could teach me . . ."

He had a feeling she was talking about more than just gambling.

After an evening—or early morning—of thoroughly enjoyable, exhausting sex—and from the sounds of it, the same thing had been going on in the next cabin, as well—the killer lay next to her sleeping sex partner, wondering if she should kill him.

What would it accomplish? she wondered.

She fell asleep before she could decide.

TWENTY-EIGHT

In the morning Clint woke with Wendy curled up next to him, warm as a kitten. Remembering the night they'd had together, he figured that if she took to gambling as well as she took to sex, she'd be unbeatable.

He tried to rise without waking her, but she reached for him as soon as he moved his legs.

"It's morning," he said.

Her hand closed over him and she said, "Lessons aren't over . . ."

She reached up and curled her hand around the back of his neck and tugged his head down so that it was nestled between her legs. He didn't bother trying to resist. He had discovered the joys of Wendy Warren, and he was fascinated by her. She arched her hips to meet the pressure of his mouth, and he tasted her sweetness, lapping at her as if she were the only breakfast he was going to get.

Hartman woke to find Fay back down between his legs again, using her mouth to arouse him and awake him.

"There you are." She was looking at him from next to

139

his swollen penis, which—glistening from her saliva—prodded at her chin.

"Good morning," he said.

"Not yet," she said, climbing astride him and engulfing him, "but it's gonna be!"

A half hour later Rick Hartman left his cabin on shaky legs and walked unsteadily to the gaming car. When he got there, he found that somehow it had been transformed into a dining car, and most of the customers were there having breakfast.

Most of the customers and Clint Adams.

Clint spotted Hartman as soon as he walked in and motioned for him to join him.

"Sam will take your order."

"How did they do this?"

"I don't know, but it changes back at noon, so eat what you can."

"Luckily," Hartman said, eyes gleaming, "I managed to work up an appetite."

"So did I."

"I don't know how you did it," Hartman said, "but I did it the old-fashioned way."

"Got along with Fay, did you?"

"Well, we did have to share a bed, so we made the proper adjustments."

"I know," Clint said, "I heard. You sounded like a wounded buffalo."

Hartman gave Clint a serious look and said, "I felt like one. I don't know how much truth we've been hearing since Rogers showed up dead, Clint, but one thing is for sure. That girl is a pro!"

"I see. What you did you did in the name of truth and justice."

"That's right. My body was all I had to give, and I gave it willingly. By the way, what about Wendy Warren?"

"What about her?"

"You still going to give her lessons?"

Clint refrained from saying that that was what he'd spent the night doing and said instead, "I'll have to see."

"I mean, I'd be glad to stand in for you."

"Don't you ever get enough?"

"Always ready for something different, Clint. Fay is a seasoned veteran, while Wendy looks like she might just be starting out. Might be interesting to compare."

"Well, take your best shot and see what happens."

"I appreciate that."

"Don't mention it."

"You're welcome to try Fay if you like—not that we've ever shared a woman before—"

"And we won't now," Clint said. He meant Wendy, but he was sure Hartman thought he meant Fay. "Besides, from the sound of you last night, I'm afraid she'd kill me. Give me a heart attack or something."

"Well, she'd sure as hell try."

"I'll leave a pro like her to a younger man like you."

"Ha!" Hartman said, all of five years younger than the Gunsmith.

Sam came to take Hartman's order and somehow worked it out so that he brought both of their breakfasts at the same time.

When they were done and Sam was clearing the dishes, Clint asked, "Sam, have you seen Mr. Hargrove this morning?"

"Not yet, sir. It's strange, too."

"Why's that?"

"He's usually the first one in here in the morning to supervise things."

"And you haven't seen him at all today?"

"No, sir."

Clint and Hartman exchanged glances, and then both rose and hurried from the car. They ran through the livestock car, surprising Jack as they did, and burst into the car that housed the office. There, standing in the hall, was Sid Borden.

"Sam . . ."

"Good morning, Mr. Adams—"

"Have you seen Mr. Hargrove this morning?"

"No, I haven't. Kind of strange, too, 'cause he's usually up pretty early. Mr. Rogers was always the late sleeper—"

"Do you have your keys?"

"Yes, sir."

"Let's open Mr. Hargrove's cabin."

"You don't think he's—"

"Let's just get it open and see, okay?"

Borden fumbled for his keys, found the right one, and slipped it into the lock. When he turned it, they entered without knocking, and a startled Hargrove sat straight up in bed and shouted, "Don't kill me!"

"Nobody's going to kill you, Ernie," Clint said.

Hargrove lowered his hand from his defensive posture and asked, "What the hell is going on?"

"You slept late, Ernie, and everyone was worried," Hartman said.

"You mean . . . you thought I'd been killed?"

"We were just concerned."

"Oh, my God. I slept late!" Hargrove said, looking at the time. "It's ten o'clock. I've got to supervise the breakfast—"

"Everything's been done, Ernie. Relax," Clint said. To Borden, he said, "You can go outside, Sid. Thanks."

"Sure." To Hargrove, Borden said, "Glad you're all right, Mr. Hargrove."

"Uh, yeah, sure, thanks, Borden."

After Borden had left and closed the door behind him, Clint said, "I've got more questions for you, Ernie. You can answer them while you get dressed."

"Yeah, sure," the man said, swinging his legs around to the floor and rubbing his face. "I've never slept late before. I must be more upset than I thought."

"Uh-huh. Look, Ernie, I want to be frank. More and more we've been hearing about trouble between you and Rogers. You want to tell me about it?"

Hargrove poured some water from a pitcher into a basin and said, "All right. Yeah, we were having problems. It's like a marriage that goes stale after a while. We just couldn't work together anymore. We were gonna approach the people back East and tell them to pick one manager, either John or me."

"And now that he's dead, there's no chance that they'll pick him over you."

Hargrove turned, his face dripping, and stared at Clint with his mouth open. "Are you trying to prove that I killed him? I thought you said a woman killed him."

"I'm not trying to prove anything, Ernie. I'm just trying to gather all the facts—and as far as a woman killing him, that's a theory."

"So you think that maybe I worked with a woman to kill him? Like maybe Madam Cyn?"

"Madam Cyn doesn't seem to like either one of you, Ernie."

"Well, that's true." Hargrove picked up a towel and dried his face. "She hated John, but I think she only dislikes me intensely. You think maybe she did it?"

"What would she have to gain?"

"John wanted to have her replaced."

"John did."

"Right."

"Not you?"

"Hell, no. She may be a bitch, but she does a good job."

"Why did Rogers want to have her replaced."

"I think he was complaining that she wasn't sending him her best girls. I also think he was trying to get her into bed, only she wasn't having any."

"So you're saying she had a motive to kill him."

"I guess that depends on just how much she needs this job."

"If she left, wouldn't she take her girls with her?"

"Some maybe, but hell, there are always girls, Clint. You know that."

So now they were on a first name basis.

"Yeah, I know that. Ernie, Rick and I are going to need our guns."

"Oh, yeah, I guess you will, seeing as how you're looking for a killer and all. The suckers aren't going to like it, though."

"If you feel you have to explain it, tell them that we joined your security force."

"Yeah," Hartman said, "tell them we tapped out and have to work our way the rest of the way—like Fay was doing."

"I'll think of something to tell them. Just tell Jack that I said it's all right. He knows about John, and he knows you're looking for the killer.''

"Okay, Ernie, thanks. See you later."

"Sure, if the killer doesn't see me first."

TWENTY-NINE

The killer left the cabin just as a woman was leaving the cabin next to it.

"Looks like those two friends both got lucky," the other woman said to the killer.

"Looks like it."

"Mine sure knew how to use his. What about yours?"

"I'd rather not—"

"Aw, hell, I embarrassed you. I'm sorry. Are you a gambler, sweetie?"

"Aren't we all?"

"Sure, I guess—hey, wait a minute," the other woman said, "Didn't I see you last night with that fella, the one that got killed? Rogers, is that his name?"

"I don't know what you're talking about."

"Sure you do, honey," the woman insisted. "You met him at the door of Madam Cyn's car. I think he was gonna go in to try one of the new girls, but you appealed to him instead. You got him out of there so fast that Madam Cyn didn't even see him. Hey, you must have been the last one to see him alive. That fella who was askin' all the questions would probably be interested in that."

"And you're going to tell him?"

"Hell, if you're not, somebody sure ought to—"

"I'm not," the killer said, putting her hand in her bag, shifting a small gun, and coming out with a knife, "and neither are you."

THIRTY

Clint and Hartman stopped to see Jack as they went through the livestock car and picked up their guns.

"God, you don't realize how naked you feel without it until you get it back," Clint said, strapping the modified Colt on.

"Can't comment on that," Hartman said, strapping his on. When he had a gun back in his saloon in Labyrinth, it was either a derringer up his sleeve or a smaller Colt in a shoulder rig. Clint had advised him to wear one on his hip while they were traveling.

"A man who looks like he's not wearing a gun is a target. If you're going to wear one, wear it in plain sight."

After they picked up their guns, they walked through the sleeper car to the gaming car, where breakfast was still going on. In fact, Wendy Warren was there having breakfast and waved to Clint as they walked in.

"The look on that little girl's face tells me I don't have a prayer," Hartman said. "Guess I'll either stick to Fay or try out Madam Cyn's."

"Sorry to disappoint you," Clint said out of the side of his mouth as they approached her table.

"Won't you gentlemen join me for some coffee?"

"A little later, maybe, Wendy," Clint said. "We've got some things to take care of."

"Are we going to continue the lessons later?" she asked.

Clint didn't know if she meant gambling lessons or sex lessons, but he said, "As soon as I get free."

"I'll be waiting."

"What things have we got to do?" Hartman asked Clint as they continued walking.

"I want to act on my theory that the killer is a woman," Clint explained.

"Which means what?"

"Which means talking to every one of Madam Cyn's girls. If it's one of them, maybe she'll get nervous and tip her hand."

"If she's a killer for hire, Clint, she's not going to rattle that easily."

"I know, but what else is there to do?"

"Well, I can think of a lot worse things to do than spending the day with a bunch of whor—uh, ladies."

"That's what I thought you'd say."

Sam was setting up his bar as they passed, and Clint stopped to say, "Sam, if Mr. Hargrove is looking for us, tell him we're in Madam Cyn's."

"This early?" Sam asked. "You fellas should give yourselves a chance to wake up before you go back to bed."

"Thanks for the advice," Hartman said. "We'll consider it."

"Come on," Clint said, tugging Hartman's sleeve.

As they entered Madam Cyn's car, they saw all of her girls seated about, most of them holding cups of coffee or tea, some of them indulging in biscuits or some other light breakfast fare. Clint vaguely remember a whore once telling him that she never ate much because she didn't want to go to bed on a full stomach.

"Well," one of the aggressive women from the night before said, approaching them, "we're not open for business yet, boys, but maybe we can work something out."

"Is Madam Cynthia around?"

"She's not awake this early."

"I'm afraid we'll have to wake her."

"She's not going to like that," the woman said. "We can work out some lower rates between you and me."

As gently as he could, Clint slipped past the woman and said, "Another time, maybe."

He walked to Madam Cynthia's cabin with Hartman following and knocked on her door.

"What?" a sleep-filled voice called out. "I'm coming."

It never occurred to Clint to call out to Madam Cyn that it wasn't one of her girls at the door. When the door opened, the woman was standing there naked, her full breasts sagging slightly, her dark brown nipples distended, a slight roll of fat visible around her waist. She looked for all the world like one of those full-bodied women you see in a painting hanging over a bar in some saloons.

She stood there staring at Clint and Hartman, not bothering to cover herself up, and said, "Is this visit really necessary?"

"It is," Clint said.

"Sorry to disturb you," Rick offered.

They entered her room. "Shut the door, will you?" she said.

He did so, and Madam Cynthia reached for her wrap and put it on. In her present blowsy state, she presented a rather slutty appearance, one that Clint found a little disconcerting.

"You just want to stare, or you want to tell me what's on your mind—and don't tell me you decided you wanted something more mature and experienced."

"No," Clint said. "I've got some bad news for you, Cynthia."

"What?"

"John Rogers has been killed."

She stared at him for a few seconds and then said, "That's neither bad news nor surprising news. I can even tell you who killed him."

"You can?" Clint said, unconsciously leaning forward.

"Sure, a woman."

Hartman said, "We've figured that much out."

"Oh, I see," Madam Cynthia said, "and you think it was me."

"No, actually we're here to question all your girls, and we'd like to use your cabin to do it in."

"You think it was one of my girls?"

"You just said it was a woman."

"Yes, but I didn't mean—all right, let me get dressed and get rid of this bed and you can use the cabin."

She reached behind her and flipped the bed up into the wall, then reached over to another wall, and pulled down her desk top. She started to remove her wrap, but then stopped and looked at them.

"You don't mind waiting outside?"

"No, we don't mind," Clint said, although he wondered what she had to be modest about all of a sudden.

THIRTY-ONE

After they had finished questioning all of Madam Cyn's girls, they closed the door of the office to discuss what they'd come up with before leaving.

"I'll tell you," Hartman said, "I've seen some ugly whores in my time, but none of these women live up to that description."

Clint had noticed the same thing. If Madam Cyn picked out her own girls, she did a damned good job of it. Even the one Clint had first thought of as fat, upon spying her fleetingly, turned out to be not fat at all, but rather quite attractive.

"I wouldn't even mind trying that big one," Hartman said. "That'd be a new experience for me. Ever had a big woman, Clint?"

"Once or twice. Can we discuss something else?"

"Huh? Oh, sure, sorry. What did we learn here?" Rick asked.

"Well, if any of these girls is lying, she's a damned good actress."

"A professional killer sometimes has to be," Rick said.

"Yeah, but all of these women alibi each other and all

their stories match. According to them, none of them left the car last night," Clint said.

"That means that if Rogers had a woman in his cabin last night, it was one of the suckers."

"There are a few women gambling out there, counting Wendy," Clint said.

"And Fay. She started this trip as a gambler."

"I guess we'll have to question them, as well."

"Wendy and Fay, too?"

"Well, we should talk to them again."

"I know how I want to divide that up."

"You take Fay," Clint said.

Hartman grinned and said, "That's what I meant."

"Let's go."

They left Madam Cyn's cabin and she was waiting outside.

"Can I have my cabin back now? I've got to get ready for business."

"Sure, it's all yours, Cynthia," Clint said. "Thanks."

"Hey," she said as they started to leave.

"Yes?"

"Is one of my girls a killer?"

"It doesn't seem that way, Cynthia," Clint said, "but keep an open mind."

"Sure. You fellas come back during visiting hours, hear? One of my girls has her eye on your good-looking friend, Mr. Adams."

"Which girl?" Hartman asked.

"Lily."

"Which one is Lily?"

"That one on the red divan," Cynthia said. Hartman looked at the red divan and saw the big woman sitting on it. She winkled at him and waved, and he waved back.

"You like big women, friend?" Cynthia asked.

"I don't know," Hartman said, "but I'm sure willing to find out."

When they entered the gaming car this time, it was once again the gaming car. The gambling was going full tilt again.

Hargrove came bearing down on them saying, "I don't think it's proper for you to be spending so much time in Madam Cyn's when there's a"—he lowered his voice—"murder to be solved."

"That's what we are doing, Ernie," Clint said, "questioning all of the girls to see who the murderer is."

"Did you find out?"

"Not yet. Now, we've got to question your female, uh, suckers."

"If you do that, it will get out."

"It can't be helped," Clint said.

"There'll be a panic."

"We hope to get it cleared up before that can happen, Ernie," Clint said because he couldn't think of anything better to say.

"Oh, all right, but not here. I'll bring them to my office one by one."

"We'll wait there."

As they passed their cabins, Clint said, "I haven't seen Fay, yet. What did you do to her?"

"Ah, I tired the poor gal out. She probably won't recover until tomorrow. I'll let her sleep a little more and question her last."

"You're so considerate."

"I know."

In addition to Wendy and Fay, there were five other female customers on the train.

There were two women together, both middle-aged and both irate at having been taken from their gambling. They said they were the Pigeon sisters, and Clint took them at their word.

There was a woman in her forties who confided that she was actually there gambling a little and looking a lot for a nice, well-to-do, middle-aged gambler for a husband. When Clint pointed out that gamblers rarely make good husbands because they aren't around a lot, she said, "I know. That figures into my plans. By the way, are you married?"

While Hartman tried to control his laughter, Clint told Sally Bailey that he was married and had five wonderful children.

"Too bad," she said wistfully.

"I know," Clint said, "we wanted ten."

The fourth female was an attractive woman in her thirties who was traveling with a male companion. He had stayed in the gaming car to gamble while she consented to being questioned. Her name was Evelyn Jones.

"I'm just along for the ride anyway, you understand. Oh, I gamble a little, but basically I'm just along for the ride."

Clint got the impression that the man was married, but that this woman was not his wife.

The last woman they questioned was a tough, mannish creature who said her name was Matilda Hemple.

"What do you think?"

"The Pigeon sisters," Hartman said. "Definite killer types. Did you see their eyes?"

"I couldn't look at their eyes; their eyeglasses were making *my* eyes water. Can we get serious about this?"

"I can't see any of those women as a killer, Clint except maybe the last one."

"I agree."

"So where are we?"

"Back to square one."

"Well, let's question Wendy next. We already questioned Fay once."

"I'll find Wendy and talk to her. You'd better go and wake Fay and see what she has to say, anyway. Maybe now that you're friends something will come out."

"Something's going to come out, all right," Hartman said, and the look on his face made it clear that what would be coming out would be from his pants.

They walked together through the livestock car and down the hall of the sleeper car. Clint left Hartman at the door of his cabin and continued into the gaming car where he found Wendy Warren playing blackjack—and winning. He was about to join her when someone came running into the car, banging into him with enough force to jar his teeth.

He turned to complain and found himself looking into the face of a shocked Rick Hartman. His face had a waxy look to it, and he had trouble getting his words out.

"Clint . . . Fay . . . my cabin—"

"Rick, what is it?"

"Fay . . . come on."

Hartman grabbed Clint's arm and dragged him back into the sleeper car and down the hall to his door.

"Inside."

Clint stared at Hartman and turned the handle on the door. He pushed it open and saw what had so shocked Rick Hartman.

On the bed, lying in a pool of blood, was Fay Gardner.

THIRTY-TWO

She had apparently been shot in the head by a small caliber gun, and this time the bullet had exited cleanly from the other side of her head, accounting for all the blood. Even a small caliber weapon made a larger exit wound than entry wound.

Clint approached the body and examined it without touching it.

Down on one knee, he turned to Hartman and asked, "Are you all right?"

"Uh, yeah, I am. It's just that this one . . . hit kind of close to home, you know? I mean, only this morning Fay and I were—"

"All right, forget about that now. Go and get Hargrove and, uh, get me Borden. Have someone else stand guard outside the office. Got it?"

"Uh, yeah, I've got it," Hartman said, but he was still staring at Fay.

"Then move!"

That galvanized Hartman into action and he ran from the cabin, slowing down only when he hit the hall. Clint reached over, closed the door, and then turned back to the body.

"All right, Fay, was it you? Did you have a falling out with your partner, or are you just an innocent victim here?"

If she was an innocent victim, then she had probably gotten in someone's way, or she had seen something she shouldn't have. Why hadn't she told them about it when they questioned her? Maybe she hadn't realized that she had seen something, and by the time she did realize it, it was too late.

The first one to arrive was Borden, who knocked on the door and stared when Clint opened it.

"Another one?"

"Killed the same way."

"During sex?" Borden asked.

Clint looked at him and then said, "I doubt it."

"Whose cabin is this?"

"My friend, Rick Hartman's."

Borden remained quiet after that, but his eyes said it all. In his view, that made Hartman a suspect, but Clint knew better.

"Stand outside, Sid, and don't let anyone in except Hartman or Hargrove."

In a few minutes they both showed up together and Borden allowed them in.

"Oh no, not another one," Hargrove said, "and a woman." Suddenly he looked as if something occurred to him. "Hey, what if she's the one who killed John?"

"Then who killed her?" Clint asked.

"An accomplice? A lover? Whose cabin is this?"

"Mine," Hartman said, "and she was alive when I left it this morning."

Hargrove looked at Hartman and then took two steps back to put more space between them.

"Shit!" Hartman said in disgust.

"Mr. Hartman is not a suspect," Clint said. "He was playing cards when Rogers was killed."

"But what about the girl?" Hargrove asked.

"He was with me at breakfast."

"What if he killed her before he left the cabin?"

"He didn't."

"How do you know?"

Clint stood up and went nose to nose with Hargrove. "Because I saw her this morning, all right?"

Hargrove blinked a couple of times and then averted his eyes. "All right, I didn't know."

Clint looked at Hartman and said, "Wendy."

"What about her?"

"She was still in the cabin this morning. We've got to talk to her."

"What am I supposed to do?" Hargrove asked as they moved to leave.

"Nothing. Leave Borden outside the door and go on about your business."

"Go on about my business? With people dropping dead all around me?"

On the way to the gaming car Hartman asked, "What do you think?"

"I don't think you did it."

"Thanks for the vote of confidence, but she's dead in my cabin. I think Hargrove knows that you're lying about having seen her—which I thank you for, by the way."

"Don't thank me," Clint said, "I'm just as sure as if I had seen her."

"Then what's going on?"

"I don't know. Either whoever killed her was after you—which doesn't make much sense—or she saw something she didn't tell us about and got killed for it."

"Why would they be after me?"

"Maybe they were after me and she saw them outside my door. Who knows? We may never know, but right now I want to find out what Wendy knows."

Wendy was still standing at the blackjack table, losing now. Clint grabbed her by the arm.

"Come on."

"But I'm losing. You said I might have to leave while I was winning, but you didn't—"

"Come on, Wendy! This is serious."

"What's serious?" she asked as he half dragged her from the car. He didn't say anything until they were in the car's alcove.

"A woman was killed this morning," Clint said, "the woman who was with Rick in the next cabin. Remember? We could hear them?"

"I remember. Killed? How? Why?"

"We don't know why, but she was killed the same way a man was killed last night."

"A man was killed last night?"

"John Rogers, one of the managers of the train. He was killed the same way the woman was—shot in the head with a small caliber bullet at close range."

"This is horrible."

"Yes, it is, but you can help."

"How can I help?"

"After I left this morning, did you see anything or hear anything?"

"Like what?"

"Like anything. Think, Wendy!"

"All right," she said, frowning. "The only thing I

heard was movement. You know, banging—like we heard this morning. I thought he was in there with her, you know, doing it again.''

"She put up a struggle, then," Hartman said. "She must have let the killer in. That means she knew him."

"Who did she know besides you and me?" Clint inquired.

"Hargrove."

"He's no killer."

"Well, neither am I," Hartman said, noticing with annoyance that Wendy, eyeing him strangely, had backed away from him.

"*I* know that," Clint said, assuring him. "Wendy, did you see anything when you left the cabin this morning?"

"No, nothing."

"Think about this, now. Was it quiet next door when you left?"

She thought back, then nodded her head, and said, "Yes, the noise had stopped. I figured they were . . . you know, sleeping." Then suddenly her ice-blue eyes widened and she said, "My God, you mean I heard that woman being killed right next door?"

"It would seem that way," Clint said.

"Clint, maybe I could have saved her," Wendy said, putting her hands to her mouth.

He took her by the shoulders and said, "And maybe you could have gotten yourself killed. Go back to the game, Wendy, and don't think about this. I'll talk to you later."

"How can I not think about it?"

"Don't think about it, and don't talk about it with anyone. Understand?"

"I understand, Clint, but—"

"Go, gamble, like a good little girl."

She turned and went through the door and into the gaming room. Clint and Hartman went through the other door and into the sleeper car.

"What's next?" Hartman asked.

"Well, I want to get the mess in your room cleaned up and move her body into the ice car with the other one. After that, I guess we'll just have to see."

"When do we hit a town next?"

"North Platte," Clint said, "midnight tonight. If we don't have it solved by then, we'll have to turn it over to the authorities there."

"And that'll be the end of Hell-on-Wheels."

"Not if we can help it."

THIRTY-THREE

If anything good came out of the two murders on the Hell-on-Wheels, it was realizing that having a doctor aboard would have been a good idea.

"I wish we had a doctor to examine these bodies," Clint said. He was talking to Hargrove and Rick Hartman while he examined the body of Fay Gardner again.

They were in the ice car where John Rogers' body was being kept underneath a tarpaulin, and they were about to cover Fay's when Clint wanted another look.

"If there's still a Hell-on-Wheels after this," Hargrove said, "I'll take care of that."

Clint thought that was sort of closing the barn door after the horses had gone, but he left that unsaid.

"What are you looking for?" Hartman asked.

"Wendy said she heard some commotion like a fight in the next cabin, right?"

"So?"

"That would indicate that Fay had resisted, put up a battle."

"What are you getting at?"

Clint turned away from the body and said, "I can't find

any signs of a struggle on the body. No bruises, no abrasions—only the gunshot wound.''

''I don't understand,'' Hargrove said.

''I think I do,'' Hartman said, but he let Clint explain himself.

''She was shot in the head at close range.'' Clint walked up to Hartman and put his forefinger against his temple. ''Would you stand still while someone shot you in the head at close range?''

''Hell, no,'' Hartman said. Then he added, ''Only if I didn't know it was coming.''

''If she didn't know it was coming,'' Clint said, turning back to the body, ''would she have struggled? And if she struggled, I would think that she would have to have been knocked unconscious before the gun could be placed right up against her head.''

''So if there was a struggle—and enough of one that Wendy heard it—she should have been knocked out during it,'' Hartman said.

''And there'd be signs of that—a bump, a bruise, a soft spot.''

''And there's none?'' Hargrove asked.

''There's none,'' Clint said. ''There is something, though.''

''What?'' Hartman asked.

''There's a small nick underneath her chin, the kind you and I get from shaving.''

Hartman thought a moment and then said, ''A knife?''

''I'd say so. I'd say somebody caught her coming out of the room, put a knife to her throat, herded her back into the room, and shot her.''

''They remained silent for a few moments while they all thought about that. Then Hargrove said, ''But what about the struggle Wendy said she heard?''

Clint and Hartman exchanged a look and Clint said, "She lied."

"Then—then she's the killer," Hargrove said.

"At the very least," Clint said, covering the body, "she has some explaining to do."

It had been an hour since Clint had told Wendy to be a good girl and go gamble. They went to the gaming car and there was no sign of her. Hargrove went to the dealers and asked if they had seen her, describing her as well as he could.

"Well?" Clint said.

"The blackjack dealer said he remembered her from yesterday and this afternoon. He said he didn't see her at his table again after you took her away."

"She was losing," Clint said. "It would be logical for her not to go back there right away. What about the other tables?"

"They've been pretty busy, but none of the dealers can remember having seen a girl of that description at their tables today."

"Where'd she go?" Hartman asked.

"If she's the killer," Clint said, "then she probably realized that we'd see through her story."

"Which means she's in hiding."

"On my train?" Hargrove asked.

"That's right, Ernie," Clint said, "it's your train. Get some of your security men and have them search this train from front to back, anywhere that you think she could be hiding."

"Right."

Clint and Hartman went back to Hargrove's office, where he found them and reported that the search was underway.

"How many men?" Clint asked.

"Six."

"How many cars are there on the train that she'd have access to?"

"Well, this car, the sleeper, the gaming car, Madam Cyn's car, the car for the high-stakes games, the livestock car, the ice car, the supply car. I guess that's it. Eight."

"No access to the engine from here?"

"Not unless she wanted to go outside the train and do some climbing."

"We'll discuss that possibility if we don't find her. Do me a favor and supervise the search, huh, Ernie?"

"Of course," Hargrove said, puffing up his chest. "We'll find her, Clint, and I'll bring her to you."

"Fine."

After Hargrove left, Hartman looked at Clint and said softly, "You really think it's her?"

"It makes as much sense as anything, I guess. Lord knows she doesn't know how to gamble, so what was she doing on this train unless it was to kill someone like John Rogers?"

"Hired by that gal in Omaha?"

"That's for the authorities to find out."

"She seemed to be so surprised, so shocked when we told her—"

"A pro would be a good actor, Rick. It's part of the job."

"What if she's got an accomplice after all, Clint? He or she could be hiding her, maybe in one of the cabins."

"You've got a point." Clint stroked his jaw for a few seconds, thinking, and then asked, "Is Borden still outside or did Ernie take him on the search?"

Hartman looked out in the hall, and when he told Clint

hat Borden was there, Clint got up and they went out into
he hall.

"Sid, do you have keys to all the cabins?"

"Sure."

"All right, we're going to search them."

"Whatever you say," Borden agreed. He had obviously come to consider Clint as the man in authority over
Hargrove.

"What are we looking for, Mr. Adams?"

"A killer," Clint answered, "a killer."

THIRTY-FOUR

There were a dozen cabins in the sleeper car and, with gambling at its height, the chances were good that most of them would be empty.

But not the first one they checked.

When they opened the door, the two people on the bed sat up, startled. Clint immediately recognized Evelyn Jones, who was much more attractive with her clothes off than she had been with her clothes on. The man in bed with her was middle-aged and balding and looked as if he might have thought that Clint and Borden had been sent by his wife.

"What can we do for you?" Evelyn Jones asked, recovering first.

"I told you we should have gambled," the man complained.

"Actually, what you're doing looks like much more fun than gambling, friend," Clint said, "considering the company you're in."

Evelyn Jones smiled broadly at Clint, becoming even prettier.

171

"We're sorry we disturbed you," he said to her
"Please, carry on."

As they pulled the door shut, he heard the man com
plaining, "I'm going to go and play cards."

"Lie back down, Walter," Evelyn Jones said. "I'r
getting on top this time. Maybe something will happen.'

They went down the line of cabins on that side of th
car, and the rest of them were empty. They checked ther
out thoroughly, disturbing them as little as possible, an
then locked them up when they left.

Next, they checked the side of the car that Clint an
Hartman had their cabins on. Likewise, they were a
empty.

"So much for that," Clint said. "I guess we'll have t
wait for the outcome of Ernie's search. Let's go back t
his office."

"You fellas feel like a drink?" Borden asked suddenly

"Sure. What did you have in mind?" Hartman asked

"I thought I'd go to the bar and get something fror
Sam."

"Good idea," Hartman said, "Why don't you get
bottle? I could use a stiff one right about now."

"Fine. I'll be right back."

They split up there, Clint and Hartman going back
the office while Borden went to the bar.

In the office they went over the facts as they knew then
with Hartman ticking them off one by one. While h
listened, Clint began going through the material in Ha
grove's desk. In a bottom drawer he found the files f
each man in the security force and just for something to d
he began scanning files.

Hargrove returned later with a negative report on th
search.

"We found nothing," he said. "Not a sign of her.

"She couldn't have just vanished," Hartman said, looking at Clint. "What's wrong, Clint?" he asked.

The Gunsmith was sitting straight up in his chair and looking at one of the security files.

"Ernie, according to this Borden was hired just before this trip."

"That's right."

"Did you check out his story about his working with Pinkerton?"

"It's being checked out, but we didn't have the time to wait for the reply. It'll be waiting when we get back."

"And it'll probably be negative."

"What's gotten into you?" Hartman asked.

"Rick, what was Borden's reason for leaving the Pinkertons?"

"He said he drank too much—same reason he failed as a fighter."

"And where did he just say he was going."

"Well, he was going to the bar to get a . . . a bottle—wait a minute."

"That's right. Why would a man who has sworn off drinking suddenly feel like a drink?"

"Wait a minute," Hargrove said. "Are you saying—"

"I'm saying that maybe Wendy Warren has an accomplice, after all."

"Now I remember!" Hartman said suddenly.

"Remember what?"

"Where I've heard the name Warren before. Years ago there was a gun for hire named Warren, but he disappeared from sight after a while."

"What was his full name?"

Hartman thought a moment, then looked at Clint, and said, "Clint, it was Sid, Sid Warren!"

● ● ●

Hartman stared at Clint and said, "Could it be a father and daughter team of killers?"

"Ernie, is there a car on this train that you didn't check?"

"Well, the engine and the security quarters."

"What security quarters?"

"We've got a separate car with cabins for the security men. They've got to have a place to live while they're onboard, don't they?"

"Ernie, Borden has a cabin?"

"Well, of course—"

"Then that's where Wendy is hiding," Clint said, coming out from behind the desk on the run. "Where is it?"

"All the way back, but the door to the car itself is locked."

"The key, Ernie."

Hargrove handed Clint a key and he started for the door, calling out to Hartman, "Let's go."

As Clint and Hartman ran out the door, Clint called back, "Get some security men and meet us there, Ernie!"

THIRTY-FIVE

As it turned out, they had to go through the ice car to get to the security car, and as they entered that car, Clint slowed their progress down.

"If she's in here, she's freezing," Hartman said.

"Let's not assume that she's not. Sid's bound to realize that he made a slip, and he'd expect us to come to the security car," Clint said in a low voice. "He knows we have to pass through this one to get to it."

"All right."

Their progress through the ice car was slow enough for them to start feeling a chill. Clint even stopped at the two bodies and checked to make sure that they were dead bodies, and not live killers lying in wait.

By the time they reached the far side of the car, their teeth were chattering.

They warmed up considerably when they exited the ice car, and Clint tried the door to the security quarters.

"It's locked," he confirmed, then producing the key. He inserted it into the lock and turned it as quietly as he could. Putting the key back in his pocket, he grasped the door handle, turned it, and pushed it open.

Immediately there was a shot, and he slammed the metal door shut as the bullet bounced off it.

"I think they're inside," he said.

"Brilliant deduction. What do we do now? They can hold us off forever."

"They don't have forever. They've got to make something happen before we get to North Platte."

"Like what?"

"They could go out the other side."

"This is the last car on the train."

"I know," Clint said, looking up. "I'm going to have to go up and over to the other side."

"Have you ever walked on top of a moving train before?"

"No, why? You want to do it?"

"Hell, no. Let's just wait until we get into North Platte and let the law get them out."

"They could decide to go out the back and jump off. I don't think they'd expect me to come in that way."

"What if the door's locked?"

"I have a key."

"What if the key doesn't fit that door?"

"I'll cross that bridge when I come to it."

There was a metal ladder on the side of the car, and he tugged on it to test its strength.

"I don't think this is a good idea," Hartman said.

"I do. Stay here and wait for Hargrove and the rest of his men. If you hear shooting inside, bust in."

"Clint—"

"Wish me luck."

"That wasn't what I was going to say, but good luck."

He slapped Clint on the back. The Gunsmith went up the ladder.

The first thing he noticed was how dark it was. He

hadn't realized that darkness had fallen already. It was darker on top of the train than he thought. The train's speed and the darkness made it impossible to see anything zipping by on either side of the train.

The next thing he noticed, as he got to the top of the car, was the wind. It roared in his ears and he had to brace himself to keep from being blown off. When he started forward, the wind at his back made the going even more precarious.

Halfway across the car, he suddenly thought of a train tunnel. If one were coming up, he'd know nothing about it until he was squashed against its side. He tried to put that thought out of his mind and kept going.

He was most of the way across and feeling as if he might make it when he slipped.

Pure and simple, his foot just went out from under him and he fell. For one brief, panic-filled moment, he was suspended in air, looking up at the night sky, and then he started to flail with his arms, looking for something to stop his fall. As he went over the edge, his fingers closed on the thin lip on the roof of the car. He felt as if his fingers were being pulled off and as if his arm were being separated from the rest of his body at the shoulder.

Hanging that way by his left hand, legs kicking, he saw only one alternative. There was a window beneath him and, trying to change the direction of his kicking legs, he struck the window with both feet, shattering it. He swung his legs inside, got hold of the side of the window, and then, with a silent prayer, let go of the roof.

Again he experienced a moment of panic as he started to fall back, but he had a tight hold on the side of the window, with his right hand on the inside. Suddenly he was sprawled on the floor of a dark cabin.

He paused for a few seconds to get his breath, lying on

the floor. His left hand hurt tremendously and he found
that he could not flex the fingers. Luckily, his right hand
was still operable.

He sat up and regarded his surrounding. He hadn't
made it to the back of the car, but at least he was inside,
albeit inside one of the cabins. He wondered if Sid Borden
and Wendy had heard the sound of the breaking glass.
He hadn't heard the glass shatter because the wind had
whipped the sound away before it reached his ears, so he
had no idea how loud it might have been inside the car.
Maybe the wind had also prevented it from being heard
inside.

He got to his feet, leaning on his left hand before
realizing it and wincing at the pain.

Allowing his left hand to dangle at his side, he went to
the door, unlocked it, and began to open it slowly. All he
could see was the other side of the hall and that didn't
help. He was most of the way back, and he had to hope
that when he stepped out—and he *had* to step out—he'd
be behind the killers and not in front of them.

A move has to be made, Adams, he told himself, so
let's make it.

He took a deep breath, threw the door open, ignored the
pain in his hand and shoulder, and stepped into the hall.

It was incredibly bright—even though the lights were
actually pretty dim—and squinting against the glare he
saw Borden ahead of him, facing the car door and standing
next to a cabin with an open door.

"Borden!" he shouted.

Borden turned slowly, as if in slow motion, his gun
already out. Clint drew, and as Borden completed his
turn, the Gunsmith fired. His bullet struck the man right in
his belly, bringing pain and shock to his face. The gu

dropped from his hand and Wendy came rushing out of the open cabin near him.

"Poppa!" she shouted.

At that moment the car door burst open, and Rick Hartman was the first man through it, gun drawn. Behind him, the door belched forth security men.

Wendy was crying, and as Hartman and the security men approached her, she turned to Clint and shouted, "You bastard!"

She had the .22 in her hand and Clint suddenly felt the darkness closing in around him. Funny, there was no pain, just a numbness in his hand and shoulder . . . and then in his head . . .

THIRTY-SIX

"And you thought she'd shot you?" Hartman asked.

"I thought I'd been outdrawn by a little girl with a .22," Clint said, shifting uncomfortably in his seat. Clint, Hartman, and Hargrove were in Hargrove's office.

"Well, luckily you just passed out, and I reached her before she could fire, anyway. How's your shoulder?"

"That's for the doctor in North Platte to say," Clint said. "Right now it feels numb."

"We'll be in North Platte within an hour," Hargrove said from behind his desk. "I can't tell you how happy I am, Clint, that you wrapped this up."

"Me, too." Clint turned to Hartman and said, "Did you get the story from Wendy?"

"Somehow she found out what her father used to do for a living, and she found it exciting. She convinced him that they should both get back into it as a team. I guess Borden—or Warren—didn't take much convincing. That was three years ago, and they'd been successful in every job up until this one."

"Were they hired by Delilah Madison?"

"Yes."

"Warren was probably already on the train when Delilah offered me the job, then? Why did she offer it to me?"

Hartman shrugged and said, "Maybe she wanted to make doubly sure it would get done. We still don't know why she wanted the poor guy killed and who knows if we ever will."

"Wendy doesn't know?"

"She says they never asked why."

"Who tried to kill us in Omaha?"

"That was Wendy's idea. When she heard from Delilah that she'd tried to hire you, Wendy figured you might become dangerous. She wanted you dead before you got on the train."

"She could have killed me last night in my cabin."

"Like I said, she wanted you dead before you got on the train. Once you were on, I guess she figured it was too chancy."

"What happened to Fay?"

"She got in the way," Hartman explained. "She saw Wendy and Rogers together the night Rogers was killed, and when Wendy found out, she just backed her into the cabin and killed her, just the way you said."

"I guess that does wrap it up, then," Clint said, shifting in his seat.

"You'd better get some rest," Hartman said. "Come on, I'll take you back to your cabin."

"And then you'll go and play some poker."

"Got to get some gambling in on the trip."

"So we're not getting off at North Platte?"

"The doctor will come on to check you out, but I figure we'll stay with the train until you heal."

"Or until you go broke."

Hartman shrugged and said, "Whichever comes first."

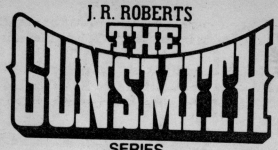

J. R. ROBERTS
THE GUNSMITH
SERIES

Prices may be slightly higher in Canada.

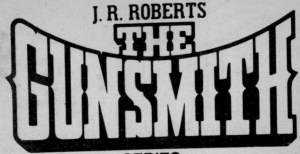

J. R. ROBERTS
THE GUNSMITH
SERIES